A Sucker for Christmas

Christmas
Tinsel & Tentacles
JP Sayle

Story Outline

An annual Christmas vacation to Australia gives two long-term friends more than they bargained for—love. But one of them has a secret that could suck in more ways than one.

Fitch found his soulmate, Shaun, when they were both four years old, but they were separated by two things, a couple of oceans and their age. Not to mention the secret Fitch has been keeping. The fact you can turn into an octopus at will isn't the kind of thing to be sprung on anyone, especially a soul mate.

Every winter, Shaun heads down under to spend Christmas with his family. For the last twenty years, he's spent his favorite holiday surfing and lazing around on golden beaches with his best friend, Fitch. Shaun wants more than friendship, however, but has no clue how to get the man of his dreams to see him as more than a friend. Enter Mandy, Shaun's sister, and Christmas is all set to become an adventure with hilarious consequences.

Fitch and Shaun are about to find out how to deal with the discovery that true love comes with suckers.

Dedication

No author is alone on the road (or sea journey), my grateful thanks got to my team, Guy, Virginie, Hannah, Julie and of course my other half Mandy who is the voice of reason in my head.

I thank each and every reader who picks up my books and gives then a go. You are what makes my dreams become a reality :)

Contents

Prologue

Fitch

Byron Bay 2012

The sun bounced off the sea, making it sparkle and drawing me to the water's edge. I ran down the sandy beach kicking sand everywhere at the unsuspecting people, enjoying the morning heat before it got hotter than hell. My gaze caught on to the person I'd spent the last eleven months thinking about seeing again. Shaun.

"Fitch, hold up. I need a hand hauling all this stuff as your dad is busy teaching."

I didn't slow at the call from Mom and pretended I'd suddenly gone deaf. Instead, I picked up speed at the lure of the warm ocean against my body and the boy waving at me in the distance, all enthusiastic.

Shaun's wide and happy smile, even with the gap between us, set my pulse tripping over itself just like my feet in my haste to get to him. My entire year got focused on this month, December, when I got to spend thirty-one days with Shaun. Got to do all the things I imagined for months.

He towered over me, and his longer limbs made him gangly next to me. He still hadn't quite grown into his body. Had he grown taller? His shoulders were filling out. I could see all the changes

I'd not noticed on the small screen of my iPad when we chatted via messenger. And he normally had more clothes on than just the red swimmers he currently wore. My mouth dried at how they hung off his lean hips and stopped just above his knees, revealing lily white skin that I knew would be nearly as tanned as mine after a month.

Last year, when puberty hit, so did all the thoughts about what it would be like to be able to touch all that milky white skin. My lips puffed out and I picked up speed, wanting to get to him, eager to be near him. The time we spent apart had gotten harder for me to cope with, though it was how I'd discovered our genuine connection.

At four, I'd become aware of two things; I could shift into an octopus, and Shaun was my soulmate. I'd never shared either of these facts with the boy who seemed just as keen to get to me as he loped towards me. I figured if he knew about me, he'd swim back to England to avoid the crazed dingo spouting crap. That first meeting, when he'd got separated from his parents on the beach and I'd been having a meltdown in the sea when my hands had formed into tentacles, had stayed with me. It had gotten etched inside my brain and he'd wormed his way into my heart when he'd asked me if I was alright, despite being just as upset as me.

It was Shaun all over; he was caring and thoughtful. He some-how distracted me enough to stop crying. Shaun hadn't seemed to notice the tentacles where my fingers had been. He'd slung his arm around my shoulders and told me he'd help me. In the end, I helped him find his parents. At that moment, my four-year-old heart had been lost to him. It was as simple as that.

Eleven years later, that hadn't changed. I'd gone through tough times while I'd considered there was something wrong with me, when I didn't understand what it was about the golden-haired boy that made me feel complete. At four, I wasn't equipped to have a conversation with my parents about these things. Heck, I wasn't now, at fifteen, with all the raging hormones that came at thoughts of Shaun in swimmers. There was no way I was gonna talk about the regular boner I got for Shaun in the middle of the night when my head and heart engaged. But I talked about the other stuff... sort of. And at age eleven, after another meltdown at Shaun leaving me, my parents had made sense of what had happened. Soul mates. We were soul mates and Shaun didn't have a clue—or about what I was.

My father was like me, an octopus, whereas Mom was human with *no extra bits*, as Dad called them. She had accepted Dad with no problem, or that's what they told me. I figured there had to be a little freak out. Surely?

I staggered to a halt in front of Shaun, chest heaving, flushed and sweating from the exertion, and grinned stupidly at him, unsure of my moves. My hands balled into fists at the urge to reach out.

His smile stretched wide, and he looked me up and down, appraising me in a way that told me he missed nothing. My boy was observant.

"Hey numbnuts, why you lookin' at me like I've grown two heads?" Shaun's voice was rough with emotion and sent shivers through me. His hand went to his chin and rubbed at it when I couldn't find something to say, too distracted by how much I wanted to wrap my arms around him. Last year, he'd had an outbreak of teenage spots that had made him spend too much time looking down and acting all kinds of awkward around me. This year, his skin was flawless, adding to the hotness factor.

"Nah, one ugly head's enough to look at. Who'd wanna see two of ya?" I joked, purposely glancing sideways to where his twin sister, Mandy, sat on the sand with Shaun's parents. They were under an enormous umbrella and she was giving them a look of disdain only a girl could give.

Shaun held up his fist for a knuckle bump and laughed hard enough his body shook. "Good one!"

"Fitch," said Mom in a frustrated tone that spoke to the level of peeved she was. "Ya could have helped carry some of this gear that ya insisted ya needed."

At the reprimand in her tone, I turned to face her and gave an apologetic smile. "Sorry," I mumbled and grabbed the large esky from her. I dumped it next to where Mandy remained, giving me death glares when I sent sand flying all over her beach towel and legs.

This earned me a narrow-eyed look from Mom that warned of retribution. I dropped my gaze, shoulders sagging under the weight of her stare.

"I see your dad is teaching surf lessons today." Shaun tugged on my hand, his fingers remaining clasped around mine as he dragged me to where Dad was, down at the far end of the beach. "Do you think he'll give me a couple of free lessons?" The grin he aimed at me sent a flood of hormones through me and my shift was hard to hold back.

Being a teenager came with a big downside. Pesky hormones. They wreaked havoc on my control, and I had to breathe slow and even, while tugging my hand from Shaun's. It was the last thing I wanted to do but going all tentacles on him wasn't part of my vacation plans. It was a reminder that I gave myself every year, which I never seemed to listen to. The older I got, the harder it was not to share what I was with him.

He eyed our separated hands with a look of hurt shadowing his eyes.

I hated that I'd put it there, so I made a big show of wiping the hand he'd held down my swimmers. "Sweaty mate, aww gross!"

He came at me with both hands and went to rub them on my chest, but I jumped back, heart skittering inside my ribcage like a freshly fired pinball. My feet sank into the wet sand, and I staggered, falling back into the unexpected wave that hit my legs. I surfaced from the water, purposefully coughing up a lung. I'd learned fast that he was too observant to not act the way normal folks would in the salty water.

He creased up with laughter, bent over, body shaking.

I put my hand under the water and, not overthinking it, I shifted my hand into tentacles and reached for Shaun's ankle. Quick as a flash, I dragged him into the water when I could see no one was paying us any attention. I'd timed it perfectly and his eyes widened right before he landed with a big splash as the next large swell hit us.

When he surfaced, coughing and spluttering next to me, I grinned at him.

His hands dragged through the tangle of wet hair now plastered to his face. "Dude! What was that?"

I got up and went to offer him a hand when he got caught out by the next wave and floundered, dunking back under the water.

Water streamed down his chest as I easily hauled him up, despite our size difference. He might have been bigger than me, but I was much stronger. Octopuses could lift twenty times their body weight. Sometimes it was cool to be different.

"Ya got hit by the surf monster. He likes to sucker ya into the surf," I joked with him, like I'd always done when I'd used a tentacle to touch him. With how I struggled to actually say the words aloud, I thought maybe that could be a way to show him what I was.

He eyed the sea like he'd done a thousand times when I joked about sea monsters, unsure what might lurk beneath the waves. Folks from England were always worried about sharks and shit like that attacking them.

He continued to hold my hand, this time dragging me out of the sea, making me chuckle. "If ya wanna surf lesson, ya know it involves water? Ya might be better with a boogie board to lie on. Seems as ya can't stay on ya feet." I nudged him with my shoulder, and my breath caught at the feel of wet, silky skin brushing against mine.

"Dick." He scowled, but his eyes were gleaming with amusement. "Not all of us have a beach and surf on our doorstep all year round," he said, continuing to move us clear of the water. "And you gotta stop that shit 'bout surf monsters. There's all kinds of weird shit in the sea, like... like... octopuses. Those things creep me out with all their suckers and tentacles."

He shivered, so I slung an arm around his shoulders and tugged him into my body even as he cut at my heart with what he'd said. He stilled when lots of wet skin pressed together. Our gazes locked and something passed between us that made the air fizzle around us. The dark blue of his eyes appeared black as his pupils dilated. Could he feel the connection between us? I sure as heck could, but his words hung between us like a barrier. One I was never going to be able to remove because I couldn't change who I was.

It was hard to resist the temptation to lean in and taste his full lips. To prove him wrong about how cool an octopus could be. Someone bumped into us and Shaun twisted away, a blush coating his cheeks as he gave me a sheepish smile.

I glared at the guy who gave us a wave of apology before heading up the beach carrying a surfboard. I told myself it was a relief to no longer be touching Shaun, and if it was a lie, no one had to know but me.

Chapter One

Mandy (Games afoot)

Byron Bay 2023

I waited until Fitch's parents sat down on the sofa, drinks in hand, before I stood in the middle of the room. I took a deep breath and smiled reassuringly at them and at both of my parents, who I'd encouraged to invite Kasey and John over for a barbeque. My palms were a little sweaty as I jumped in with both feet. "I think we need to do an intervention for Fitch and Shaun."

"An intervention?" asked Mom, her slim brows rising as she glanced at Dad and then gave a worried look at Kasey and John. "I don't think that's a good idea."

"You know about Fitch," I accused, because everything about the way the four people in front of me were behaving suggested that they were aware of Fitch's... other side.

I'd had years to adjust. At fifteen, I'd been watching Shaun and Fitch messing in the surf. Initially, I thought I was mistaken when Shaun fell into the water and I'd noticed something unusual coming from Fitch's hand. Later, at sixteen, having been watching Fitch like a hawk, I'd discovered it was indeed tentacles. Then I'd waited for there to be some kind of big reveal but only got crickets.

Watching both Shaun and Fitch circle each other like sharks sniffing out blood had been fun for the first couple of years. It was so old now. Neither seemed capable of making a move and as Shaun's big sister, and someone who considered Fitch like a brother, I felt it was my duty to give him a good kick up the ass to get him moving in Fitch's direction.

"Know what, dear?" answered Mom in a neutral tone that belied the nervous tension in her eyes.

"Mom, I'm twenty-five years old. I'm not a kid who can't tell when you're not being truthful with me. You brought us up to always tell the truth," I pointed out, knowing just where to hit.

She winced and took a deep swallow from her wine glass.

"What do ya think you know?" questioned John, looking relaxed on the sofa, arm flung along the back, holding a stubby.

"That Fitch has tentacles," I said, holding John's stare. There was a choked sound before Dad was up and slapping Mom on the back as she coughed.

John's expression never changed, though there was a stillness about him that suggested I'd thrown him for a loop. "Have you mentioned this to anyone?"

I'd given a lot of thought about how to broach this subject as December drew closer and brought with it Shaun's return for the holidays. I couldn't stand another year of watching Fitch and Shaun pretend there wasn't something going on between them besides being best friends. There was no issue for me over the fact Fitch was different.

As I eyed his parents, I considered how best to answer. "No, not even Shaun, and I'm pretty sure Fitch hasn't let on about what he's capable of. Not that I'm exactly sure what that is. When Shaun finally yanks his head out of his ass about Fitch, I need everyone to be on board. My twin is an annoying pain in my ass, but I love him and want nothing more than for him to be happy. Same for Fitch. He came into our lives at four and made himself right at home. There is something special about him and how he is with Shaun."

"Nicely put." Kasey nodded at me with a look of approval. "You're right. Fitch and Shaun are soulmates."

That threw me and I went to sit down next to Dad, who'd returned to his seat. Dad didn't appear at all shocked. "Wow." It was time to fish! "What is he?"

John looked at his wife and something passed between them. Seconds stretched as no one said anything. "He's an octopus," he eventually murmured, his gaze coming back to me. "So am I. I trust ya to keep our secret."

The air got caught somewhere in my throat, so I nodded emphatically, waiting for the air to leave so I could croak out a 'jeez' like a total moron.

Dad laid his hand on my knee and squeezed gently. "John and Kasey were up front with us when we moved here permanently. Fitch hasn't told Shaun... yet."

"What's holding him back?" I asked, already guessing it was several things. One being the distance between them, and possibly Shaun's dating history. I was pretty sure he'd not noticed that he dated men who were paler versions of Fitch.

"Fitch has this romantic notion that Shaun will feel the connection between them," Kasey supplied.

"Only issue with that is they've such a solid friendship. I suspect Shaun might not want to mess that up by adding romantic intentions and risk possible failure in the future." This came from John and by the expression Kasey wore, she didn't appear to agree with him, though she stayed quiet.

"That's normal." Wasn't it?

Kasey shook her head, her attention remaining on John. The love they shared was there for all to see. "Soulmates, once they connect...nothing can break them apart, not even death. It's an eternal thing."

"Lucky bastard," I muttered without thinking and got a hard stare and a loud 'tut' from Mom. "Sorry." I offered an apologetic smile, returning my attention to Kasey. "That sounds pretty awesome to me."

"It is. But Fitch has gotten into a rut. Something happened a few years back." Her smile dimmed. "Shaun made a comment about octopuses and it stuck in Fitch's head. He's scared that Shaun will reject him when he knows the truth about him. John's family has a rare genetic component that gives them an animal spirit. We haven't met another of his kind outside of John's family."

Another of those loving looks passed between them and I shifted in my seat, a little uncomfortable at how open they were with their feelings. We were British and expressing emotions wasn't the done thing.

"So how do we get them both to see sense? I don't know about you guys but I can't watch another scene of unrequited love from the Notebook play out in front of me."

Kasey's blond hair shifted around her shoulders as she tilted her head and gave me a searching stare. "Do you have some ideas to help them?"

I rubbed my hands together and grinned wickedly at them all. "A few. I think it's time to confront Fitch and also yank his head out of the sand. Shaun isn't heading home after the holidays.

He's got a job in Kemps Creek and from what I can tell as yet, he's not told Fitch."

"So, how do ya want us to help? I'm assuming that's why ya asked us around." John sipped at his stubby, wearing a grin that matched mine.

"It's time to fish or cut bait!"

Mom groaned. "How long have you been holding on to find the right moment to say that?"

Seeing some confused expressions, Mom went on to explain, "It's from Three Men and a Little Lady, one of Mandy's favorite films."

Laughing at the range of expressions, I said, "It fits, right? Anyway, here's what I think we should do..."

Chapter Two

Shaun

Exiting Ballina Byron Gateway Airport, it was easy to spot my parents' old ute. Expecting to see Dad, I groaned at the sight of Mandy in the driver's seat. I cursed under my breath at thoughts of her awful driving as I lopped over, lugging my backpack on one shoulder. My eagerness to exit the airport took a solid dive as the heat and the fatigue from the flight hit with my fleeing thoughts of napping on the way home. With Mandy driving, there was no way I was going to relax enough to sleep.

Sweat slid down the center of my back by the time I'd thrown my pack into the bed of the ute and hopped into the too hot cab. Another thing, she hated air con. I didn't get how she didn't just melt into a big puddle.

"Please tell me the air con is going on," I said in the way of a hello.

"So nice to see you too, baby brother," she quipped back, her tanned face looking healthy next to my pale complexion.

She barely gave me time to reach for the seatbelt before she took off, merging with traffic.

I gave her a death glare, one I'd learned from her. Not that she noticed as she zipped down the streets as I grabbed for the 'oh shit' bar.

The cowbag knew I hated it when she called me 'baby brother'. There were seven minutes between us, and she never let me forget she was older than me. In her head, that made her the boss of me. It was a bone of contention between us that never got old.

I smirked at her, keeping my eyes from the road she was hurling down way too fast for my liking. "You do realize that will always make me the baby of the family and you, the old hag."

Although, I hated to say that she looked younger, not that I'd ever tell her that, as I'd never hear the end of it. It was my job to rag on her, she was my sister. She'd emigrated to Australia three years before and I hated her for it.

A hand came off the steering wheel, and she aided in shoving my fast beating heart into my throat when it waved about along with the ute. "Is that the best you can come up with?"

"With how my life is hanging in the balance with your driving, yes!"

The screech of tyres as she went around the next bend got my eyes shutting and my fingers tightening on the bar I held. "This isn't the Moto GP races, those are held up in Melbourne!"

"Why so pale 'baby brother'?"

I lifted my middle finger, still with my eyes closed, and gave her the bird. This got a deep belly laugh that didn't help when I'd visions of her crashing as she shook with laughter.

"Slow the fuck down!" I demanded through gritted teeth as my body slammed into the door panel and I wrenched my shoulder, trying to keep hold of the bar above my head.

"So dramatic. With your love of motor sports, I thought you'd be much more of a speed demon rather than Driving Miss Daisy." Her amusement came across in the sarcasm I was used to, and I peeled open one eye, then promptly shut it when it appeared we were about to mount the car in front of us.

I counted the seconds in my head, aware of how long it took to get to our home. They were twenty-nine of the longest minutes of my life, thanks to Mandy!

When we finally came to a shuddering stop, my clothes were stuck to me with sweat. The hand holding the 'oh shit' bar had gone numb and refused to let go. Shaking my arm sent pins and needles along the nerve endings, forcing me to release the bar and rub at it. The breath I released was all relief at having made it in one piece to the house my parents had bought as a holiday home twenty-one years ago and moved into permanently when they'd retired fifteen years later.

The feeling of coming home never failed to surprise me as I stared at what was home every Christmas for the last two decades. I'd stayed in London when my parents had opted to move into the house here. At nineteen, I'd already started my Masters in marine biology and I'd not wanted to jump through all the hoops trying to transfer. So I'd stayed put and then went on to gain my doctorate, wanting to go into the research field. And I'd landed my dream job in Kemps Creek as a research scientist, which was less than an eight-hour drive from Byron Bay. For me, it would be like traveling from London to Scotland, meaning I'd be close to my family but far enough away to have space. They could be a little too interested in my life sometimes.

Mandy didn't make any move to get out of the ute as she turned to face me. "You're such a big baby, you know that?"

"Give over. And how many times do you need to call me a baby to get it out of your system? And just a little FYI, I wasn't the one who cried when Bambi's mother got murdered!"

She stuck her nose in the air and sniffed indignantly, her shoulder length hair swaying about her bare shoulders. The color was lighter than mine thanks to all her time in the sun. "That's 'cause you ain't got a heart."

The door beside me opened and Dad's craggy, smiling face appeared in the cab, bringing with it a wall of heat I'd stopped noticing while fearing for my life. "Are you two going to sit out in this heat all day?"

"Why didn't you come and collect me?" I asked while releasing my seatbelt, desperate to get out of the sweatbox now Dad had brought it to my attention. I was cooking in the tin can. Although I'd shoved my winter jacket in my backpack before I'd exited the airport, I still had on my hoodie and a long-sleeved T-shirt beneath. When I'd left England the day before, it had been minus four and I was always cold on the flights with the overuse of air con.

"I had some jobs your mom wanted me to do. Mandy was happy to go and collect you."

"More like come to torture me," I muttered under my breath, getting out and rolling my stiff shoulders as I breathed in the hot, scented air. Sea and flowers that I couldn't name that Mom planted on the large sloping garden that led up to the two-story house, gave me a deep down contented feeling that was only matched by...

"I wondered when ya'd get your lily white ass here."

My heart raced and the heat of the day paled compared to what ran through me as I swung around to greet my best friend, Fitch. My tongue glued itself to the roof of my mouth at the hotness that was my friend. Although he wasn't overly tall, like me, his presence seemed to fill the surrounding space, making everything else seem insignificant.

As seemed typical for him, his chest was bare and his traditional swimmers hung low, revealing cum gutters I'd had fantasies about. His skin was a deep golden brown and smooth as silk. It fascinated me how his hairless body never felt scratchy from regrowth.

Thongs slapped on the concrete as he came towards me, his fist raised for our traditional knuckle bump. The barest touch of skin sent desire through me. My cock responded and thickened, something that made me grateful for my jeans. The reaction wasn't uncommon and over the years had grown in strength. I shifted and hoped no one noticed my reaction to him. The first meeting was always the worst after such a long gap.

When I managed to swallow and get my tongue to work, I grinned at him. "Look what the cat dragged in. I thought you said you weren't due back from the trip up north until Saturday?" Fitch was a deep-sea diver and had been working in Queensland for the last six months. He wasn't supposed to be back for another three days. Not that I minded in the slightest. Fuck no, I wanted to spend every damn waking moment with him... and the sleeping ones, too. Only problem with that, I lived too far away—or had—to go after the one man who'd starred in every fantasy I'd had since I'd realized I was into boys.

"As if he could keep away from you. You're like damn magnets drawn together by the universe. Two souls..."

I didn't have time to figure out what was up with Mandy's strange waffling when Fitch's skin darkened with color before he spoke. "My boss miscalculated my vacay time and it seems I had some extra days due to me." He slung his arm around my waist in a familiar move. The scent of the sea clinging to his warm skin. He was at least a foot shorter than me, yet he always appeared bigger when he touched me. "And as ya moaned 'bout me not being here, I drove through the night to get here at the same time as ya."

Mandy's laughter was the kind that suggested she knew something I didn't as I walked off towards the house and Dad grabbed my backpack out of the bed of the ute.

As much as I didn't want to pull away from Fitch, I followed Dad. "It's heavy. I'll grab it."

Dad and Mom had started a family later than most, in their mid-forties, having said they'd sowed their wild oats first. Not something I'd wanted to think about when it came to my parents sowing oats of any kind or what they meant by 'wild'. He hefted up the backpack easily and arched his brows as he swung to face me. "You wouldn't be insinuating that I'm old and frail?"

"As if," I answered, matching his smile before he turned away, following Mandy up to the house. At nearly seventy, he cycled and surfed every day, weather permitting. Sometimes I thought he was fitter than me.

An arm slipped back around my waist and a hand squeezed my hip in a friendly manner. One I was used to, though that didn't help where my mind went. It headed straight for a gutter at the press of all the naked skin against my clothed body. How hot I was getting had nothing to do with the big, bright ball of yellow in the sky. If I could have wished my clothes right off me, fuck, I would have.

"So, ya wanna go for a 'dip'?" Fitch questioned with a sexy grin, making his features even more compelling, causing me to lose my train of thought for a second.

"Look at you being all English." I'd been teaching him for years how to talk British. It was fun listening to his Aussie accent saying British words.

His hip bumped into me and a cheeky wink chased it. "I have this bossy teacher who rags on my ass when I get it wrong. So ya gonna get changed or shoot the breeze in forty degree heat?"

I reluctantly slipped from his hold, nodding. "A swim would be great."

"At least say hi to your mom before you disappear," Dad called from halfway up the slope.

"Will do," I answered, slipping my arms out of my hoodie to pull it over my head.

"Fuck, look at those guns!" Fitch said, sounding breathless.

Head tucked in my hoodie, I couldn't see his face. I tugged it off as fast as I could and looked at my best friend. Was I picking up interested vibes from him?

Scrutinizing his expression, it was neutral and revealed none of his thoughts. I shook off the odd feeling of wishful thinking.

Friends.

We were just friends.

Nothing more...

Then why did it always feel like more when we were together?

It was damn confusing.

Chapter Three

Fitch

What the fuck had Mandy meant by her comment? I'd seen Shaun's confusion over what she'd said. Mandy was right, the universe had put us together. Was she joking, or did she know something? I tried hard to be careful...

I blew out a gusty breath. The moment I knew Shaun was going to be arriving earlier than me, I'd worked to get home as soon as possible. Nothing had changed between us, sadly, but that didn't mean I was going to miss a minute of the time he was here.

Opting to make my expression as neutral as possible, I worked on keeping my gaze from traveling over the long-sleeved T-shirt that hugged his chest and arms like a second skin. One I really wanted to replace with my body. The 'we're friends' mantra I'd adopted after his reaction to octopuses eleven years earlier got harder and harder to maintain. Every year, the need to pounce on him and make him see that I was his, that octopuses weren't creepy or scary, or that we could be fun and inventive with tentacles, grew stronger and stronger.

I'd make a dope boyfriend... with a little experience, for sure. I, unlike Shaun, hadn't got into the dating pool. He was my soul mate, and my animal side wasn't interested in anyone but the gorgeous boy who'd become a stunning man.

There'd been a tough conversation about sexual orientation when we'd turned sixteen. He'd confessed first to liking boys, and it had been a relief to talk freely about being gay right until he'd mentioned about a boy in his school he was interested in.

Since then, he'd tormented me with his relationships, not that there'd been many when he'd focused hard on studying. But the last one had lasted longer than the others and I'd feared Leo would arrive with Shaun for this Christmas vacation with us.

He'd not mentioned Leo in the last few calls we'd had and I secretly hoped that was because their relationship was over. It was selfish wanting him the way I did, I knew it, but there was little I could do about it. So instead, I acted like my heart wasn't breaking as he talked about things he did with guys that weren't me.

And it seemed the torture was going to continue because I'd not kept my big mouth shut when he'd started taking off his hoodie. Now he was laughing and flexing his arms after dropping the hoodie to the ground, as if he wanted me to drool all over his fit body.

He doesn't know you like him, so how can he be doing it to make you drool?

My octopus had recently tired of waiting and was getting very mouthy.

Slap a tentacle over your mouth.

The following silence came with a tingling in my limbs.

Don't you dare. He'll run screaming and we'll never get a chance to show him what he's been missing out on.

Nothing is what he's been missing out on, because you haven't grown a pair of balls.

Funny.

A hand touched my tingling arm and, realizing I'd zoned out, I jerked back, scared there'd be some escaping suckers.

Shaun's head tilted to the side and he wore an inquisitive expression, staring at me like he was expecting an answer.

Scrabbling to come up with something, anything, I grinned like the damn fool I was. "Yeah, let's do that," I muttered, hoping that whatever it was he said connected to my earlier comment about going for a swim. He had to be jet lagged and his usual way to deal was to spend time in the water with me, lounge on the beach catching some rays, and catching up on things we'd maybe not talked about in our weekly calls. I had everything packed in my ute, ready to go. The Esky was full of cold ones and snags ready for the day.

"Did you hear what I said?"

A flood of heat filled my face and for once, I was glad of my tan to hide my embarrassment. "Is that a trick question, mate?"

He slapped my bare arm and shook his head, bending to collect his hoodie off the ground. "Come on, I think the sun has fried your brain. A person could get their feelings hurt from being ignored by their best friend. Just sayin'," he said through laughter, showing he wasn't serious.

His ass bounced in the jeans as he strolled up off towards his home and it held all my attention. "The only thing frying my brain is your ass," I muttered under my breath.

His booted foot appeared to trip before he continued on, his backside bouncing way more than it had a second ago.

Had he heard me?

Clearly he had and was taking the piss. "If ya jiggle that ass anymore, ya'll hit the neighboring fence," I said, loud enough for him to hear, adding just enough humor so he understood I was joking.

He threw a grin over his shoulder at me, not pausing. "You say the nicest things."

"What? That ya ass needs its own giant sized slingshot to hold it in check?" I returned, enjoying how we slipped back into our usual trash talking.

His whole body shook with silent laughter as he walked up the steps to the main door. A grin plastered on my face as I went after him.

Inside the house, as comfortable to me as my own home, I nodded to Shaun's mom, who was in the open-plan kitchen prepping food for Shaun's welcome home dinner. Thankfully, there was no sign of Mandy, though I knew she'd be back to snip at us. She couldn't seem to resist, even now we were all adults.

"Fitch, you staying for dinner tonight?"

My lips parted but before I could get a word out, Shaun replied, "Do Aussie rules footballers all have mullets?"

"Mate, seriously? Ya gonna dis our sporting heroes?"

He eyed me across the room, having dropped his hoodie on a chair he passed to go give his mom a kiss on the cheek. "I'm just glad you cut yours off last year." For effect, he made his whole body shudder and curled his lip up in distaste. "You looked naff and brought down my street cred. How is anyone supposed to get laid with you cramping their style?"

I burst out laughing; it was that or cry at him trying to get laid by anyone that wasn't me. 'Naff' was a word that Shaun used a lot. Though I'd never admit it, him calling me naff about my hairstyle was what got me chopping my hair.

"Look who's naff now," his mom said, tugging on the longer strands at the back of his head and giving me a quick, supportive grin. One she'd given me many times before, making me suspect she knew I had feelings for her son. "What's this? A duck's ass? They went out of fashion when God's dog was a pup."

Gasping for air as the banter continued, I had tears running down my cheeks from laughing so hard listening to them. "Duck's ass?" I spluttered through my laughter, going over to have a closer look at the back of his hair.

To his mom, Shaun pointed and scowled. "So not cool, Mom. Now I'll never hear the end of it."

I stopped next to him, working to keep my laughter from spiraling out of control again, and slung my arm around his waist. I'd not been able to reach his shoulder comfortably in nearly ten years. "We aren't ten anymore, where name calling was funny..."

The scowl got aimed at me as he went for my ribs, where I was ticklish. "Then why are you laughing, numbnuts?" His fingers dug in as his expression turned wicked and he hit my most ticklish spot.

I darted back and hit the counter with him following fast, his fingers not leaving me alone as I gasped for air, laughing while trying to avoid him. At times like these, it was like he was the one with tentacles, not me.

"How long did it take before they were all over each other? Two minutes? Mom, you owe me five dollars."

"Wait, what?" Shaun gasped, while I tried to fend him off, laughing.

Seeing this could turn in a direction I didn't want it to go, I tugged Shaun towards the hallway that led to the stairs and their bedrooms. "Don't we have plans?" I asked, cringing at my desperation seeping through when Mandy arched just one brow and gave me a knowing smile.

Shaun glanced between me and Mandy, the amusement still evident, but there was something more. Curiosity. I knew every expression he had. This one spelled trouble for me if he started asking questions. He was always like a dog with a bone when he wanted to know something. He'd not stop until he'd picked the damn bone clean. "Am I missing something here?"

"You've been missing it since two-thousand-and-three," replied Mandy as she took a seat across the counter. Her slim legs crossed, and a bare foot bobbed as she held my stare, challenging me to say differently.

Panic reared up, all her comments merging into something that caused a fiery ball of terror inside me. What had she seen back then? Was it a tentacle? Fuck, I hoped not.

Why?

Are you shitting me?

What is that even supposed to mean?

I'm not getting into this now.

I definitely needed to be on my A game with how every pair of eyes in the room were now looking at me. "Swim... beach... let's hit it..." I stuttered and barely resisted rolling my eyes at my dag behavior.

This is all your fault!

How? I'm not the one who can speak aloud and is making a fool of themselves, am I?

Sometimes, I really hated his smart mouth!

Chapter Four

Shaun

Floating on my back, letting the waves move me, I stared up at the darkening sky. It wouldn't be long before the stars came out, and the sun set fully. The sky here always appeared to be so much bigger, and the sun looked like it was getting eaten by the sea. Once, I'd told Fitch I could hear it sizzle. The memory, like so many, was sweet and way easier to recall than any other mundane thing I'd said or done because Fitch was in it.

When I'd started to plan my future, I'd come to a conclusion that ended my last relationship. I couldn't see my future without Fitch in it. That realization had got me searching for a job in Australia, though as yet I'd not told Fitch I wasn't planning on leaving after Christmas like I'd normally do. No, I'd packed up my stuff and shipped it out before I'd left London.

It hadn't been as much of a pull to leave my childhood home as I'd thought. The uni mates who'd rented rooms in the house to help pay the bills had all left to get on with their lives. I'd spent a week before coming rattling around my home, trying to assess how I felt about what was coming next. Fear hadn't come—excitement was the major thing buzzing through me. I'd got my dream job. What I needed to go with it was Fitch. I just wasn't sure how to get him with the programme or get my fears to take a back seat.

I wasn't sure when I started seeing Fitch as more than my friend, but the distance and the fact he never made a move in my direction kept me from revealing how I felt.

Why don't you make a move?

I'd have sworn the sarcastic voice inside my tired brain was all Mandy. The exhaustion sucked big time and my body was ready to quit on me and give in to the sleep it craved. Only the day had been... weird and one of the best I'd had in the last six months. The weirdness came from how much I struggled throughout the day to resist kissing Fitch. Yep, I'd been attracted to him. Now it was like the need was on steroids and was jonesing hard to get an adrenaline rush.

It was messed up when it came with having a boner half the day with the family around. Dinner had been interesting, with me spending my time making sure no one noticed. Mandy was like a hawk and missed nothing. She'd not poked her nose in, but I'd suspected it was coming with how she'd spent dinner watching us both. So I'd been relieved when Fitch had suggested an evening swim to burn off the enormous meal I'd eaten.

My thoughts rolled back to what I was going to do to change the status quo. On camera, during our video chats, I could act like an asshat and he didn't think anything of it. Up close and personal, when he was in my space—which I noticed way more than I used to—I had the urge to taste his full lips and see if they were as soft as they appeared.

Would he freak out if I laid one on him?

Of course he would, he's been in the friend zone for twenty years!

This was why I'd figured I'd never made it work with my previous boyfriends. I measured them against my relationship with Fitch—which, yeah, was fucked up. That reality made the guilt I had for not cutting my last boyfriend, Leo, loose earlier in our relationship before feelings got involved weigh that much heavier. As it turned out, his feelings were well and truly engaged and I'd hurt him when he realized he'd been nothing more than a fling. The guy had been solid and wanted nothing more than to develop a deeper connection with me. It had taken some deep thinking to get to the root of that. But no one could reach the bar set by the guy floating at my side from a very early age.

It was the worst reality when I was too chickenshit to tell Fitch how I felt. The stark truth, I was in the same position as Leo with these all unrequited feels, and that sucked.

For a time, I'd deluded myself into believing Fitch was interested when he never mentioned dating anyone, until Mandy squashed that like she'd do a bug by pointing out not everyone was like me, who tended to over share. Had I been over sharing and putting him off?

I floundered and dropped my feet onto the seabed, water splashing in Fitch's direction. His head popped up as he somehow kept his body floating. The guy had to have been a fish in another life the way he was in the water.

In the dimming light, I could see the crease between his blond brows. "What? Did a sea monster crawl up ya swimmers?"

My eyes narrowed on him at the obvious amusement and the reminder of my childhood fears about what was in the water. I moved fast and grabbed for his swimmers, sticking my hand up the baggy leg. "I'll show you a sea monster," I cackled, before the air left my chest at the silkiness of his skin.

His laughter turned into a gurgle as he became submerged in water. As usual, he never panicked, but sank to the sandy seabed and forced me to go with him. Salt stung my eyes as I blinked and held my breath. The water was crystal clear, but the dwindling light meant I couldn't see much. Then pearly white teeth flashed brightly in the water and something slipped over my back.

Not human.

Suckers!

Holy fuck!

All the thoughts fired through my sluggish mind at once and I jerked upward, not getting far with my hand caught in Fitch's swimmers. I swallowed what felt like the entire ocean. Before I could get caught in the panic, Fitch—like always—dragged me upright and slapped me on the back. His laughter got lost in the sounds of water hitting the shoreline, and my coughing fit. "Be careful, sport."

How he manhandled me so easily when I had to weigh at least nineteen kilos more than him, I'd never figure. My cock bucked at the show of strength and I was glad we were in the water and he couldn't see.

"You did that on purpose," I accused, while trying to cough up a lung full of water and get my body to behave.

He quirked up his brows with a look of innocence I didn't buy. "Did what?"

"Use seaweed or some such shit to pretend it was tentacles touching my back."

"It was tentacles." The way he said it suggested it was the utter truth.

It was hard to gauge his expression as I glanced down at the water, seeing nothing. "I think it's time to call it a night." I needed something to get rid of the extra salty taste in my mouth and to get away from the tempting man I wanted to show off my swordfish to. A chuckle rose at the memory of what Fitch had called his dick when we got a little more interested in our anatomy.

"Ya rooted? Or are ya plain scared?" he mocked, knowing my weak spot.

It took a moment to recall what 'rooted' meant to Fitch. "Yep, I'm tired and not *scared*." I stressed the latter, getting a smirk I wanted to kiss off his face. I'd outgrown my illogical fear of the things in the waters... or I told myself that. No one wanted to come face to face with a shark.

I waded out of the water to where we'd left the esky and swag that Fitch preferred to use on the beach when we came down in the evenings. There were other people lingering, making the most of the dip in temperature and the pleasant, warm water. The Australian way of life had a lot to be desired when most of it was spent outdoors.

Fitch was silent behind me as I grabbed my towel and rubbed off some of the excess water before dropping onto my swag. Rolling to open the esky and grab a stubby, I offered it to Fitch. He grabbed it and didn't bother with the towel, just stretched out on his swag. On his side, he leaned onto one elbow to face me.

Relaxed, he brought the stubby to his lips. When they parted, my breath came in short bursts, imagining him opening for a kiss. I watched intently, considering how he might taste. Salty for sure and maybe a little sweet from the pastries Mom had made for us. His throat worked. Long and graceful, his neck got my teeth aching in my gums with the idea of placing them against his pulse and... *biting*.

Shit, I must really be tired.

Why would anyone drool over wanting to taste blood?

I tried to shake off the oddness of my thoughts, continuing to stare in fascination as if I hadn't seen him before.

He dropped the stubby to the sand, and he gave a head tilt, not taking his head away from the hand it was resting on. "What's with ya? Ya actin' weird." His voice was deep and raspy, like he'd been a long-term smoker.

A shiver ran through me. Tingles ran down my spine and lodged right in my balls. To distract myself, I went with the first thing that popped into my head. "Why haven't you ever talked 'bout your boyfriends?"

Fuck it! In for a penny, in for a pound.

"Do you have a boyfriend you haven't mentioned to me?"

Wide, startled eyes locked on me like a heat-seeking missile and my pulse hit my chest wall, waiting for the incoming impact of possibly overstepping a boundary we'd somehow drawn. The hand resting on the stubby rippled in a way that didn't look... natural. "Where'd this come from? Ya never asked 'bout this shit before."

It was hard to shrug and act like I wasn't crawling out of my skin, waiting for him to answer me, while my gaze moved between his hand and eyes. "It seems I'm an over-sharer and you share shit all…" I desperately wanted a beer to wet my throat but was too afraid to move and break the sudden stare off we had going on. "So, do you have a boyfriend?"

The head shake, when it came, was minimal, but it allowed the breath I'd been unconsciously holding to release in a loud hiss. The relief was immediate, and I resisted sagging into the swag as his gaze seemed to search mine.

Tension—for the first time in our relationship—crackled between us. It crawled over my skin and lifted the tiny hairs better than any English wind could.

"Why?" fell from my lips and he sat up, breaking eye contact to look at the sea.

"Ya fishin'?" he asked in a high and tight tone, revealing how uncomfortable he was about the subject.

"Nah…" his head fired in my direction and the sizzle in his eyes pinned me in place and made me confess the truth. "I suppose I am. It never really registered until recently that you never talk about anyone you're dating. We've been sharing secrets since we were four. You know more about me than my own parents."

Well, except that I am madly in love with him… he definitely didn't know that.

"There's nothin' to share." Before I could call him out on that he was up and jerkily rolling up his swag. The stubby lay between us, almost like a symbol of the wall he erected so fast it made my head spin. "Listen, ya gotta be buggered so I'll catch ya tomorrow."

I stared wide eyed at his retreating back.

What. The. Fuck. Was. This!

Chapter Five

Fitch

Unable to sleep, I'd got up and had taken myself out down the beach. For now, my octopus was quiet. Not something he'd been when I'd left Shaun alone on the beach last night. I'd not been prepared for his questions about my dating. I thought he was building up to saying something else with the way he'd been looking at me. That I'd thought he was getting ready to lay one on me seemed stupid now. Instead, he'd blindsided me by asking about my dating history.

He was right; he was an over-sharer, and I loved that about him. Never had he been able to hold water when it came to secrets. It was a long-standing joke between us.

My gaze was on the sky, dark orange bleeding into pinks and golds as the sun bloomed into what was going to be another scorcher of a day. A light breeze came off the sea, bringing the scent of salt and seaweed. I ran my hands through the warming sand, letting it fall through my fingers as I focused on relaxing the tension rolling through me.

A few minutes later, I sensed Dad approaching before I felt his hand rest on my bare shoulder and squeeze. This far down the beach, the land belonged to us. There was no clear demarcation, but a jut of rock marked this place as private land, so I'd not bothered with clothes. My original intention was to shift and go for a swim in my animal form but my head wasn't in the right place for that. The sea could be a dangerous place when I wasn't paying close attention.

The sand at my side shifted as Dad lowered wordlessly, removing his hand from my shoulder to rest it on my knee. Being the same as me, we were more attuned to each other. I'd learned at age ten if I opened my mind I could talk to him without speaking aloud, despite any distance between us.

Whatsup?

Shaun.

His chuckle was low and not in my head. I felt him glance in my direction. "Son, when is it not 'bout Shaun?"

I glanced sideways and sighed. "You and Mom, ya make it sound so cut and dried when ya meet your soulmate. How can't he feel the connection between us?" I asked in despair.

"He can. He just hasn't figured out what it means... *yet*."

"He's had twenty years. I don't know if I can wait another twenty!" I complained bitterly, hating how I sounded when it wasn't me to be so down. But right then, I couldn't shake off the maudlin feeling. It had gotten harder to be with him and not reveal how I felt or how my body reacted to him. Last night, I'd touched him with my tentacles and been honest about it—sort of. I'd not told him the tentacles belonged to me. I'd seen the disbelief and that had made everything feel bigger and more defeating when I was trying to be open and honest about what I was.

You weren't being honest!

Please, you've already given me a headache!

I was glad when Dad carried on and I could ignore my dag animal. "Ya met him when you were four. Ya understood at an early age, he was the other part of ya soul. That perfect match. A gift. The problem is that neither of ya were mature enough to deal with that kind of connection. It's confusing things between ya. Friendship developed in its place, as neither of ya was ready for anything else. Now ya both have to navigate that. Ya know I didn't get to meet your mom until I was in my twenties, so I was more aware of how to gain her attention."

"How is this supposed to help me?" I asked, knowing he was trying to make a point, but I couldn't see what it was with my frustration levels coming off a night of no sleep, a complaining octopus and a raging boner that wouldn't quit.

"I had nothing to unpick. I could build something that was based on the attraction. We had the connection first and with that came friendship. You've done it in reverse. It's harder to move from friendship when Shaun could perceive he's a lot to lose if things went wrong between ya."

"Nothing will go wrong between us!" I snapped.

His laughter rumbled out of him and his eyes crinkled at the edges in amusement. "You know that, he doesn't. How can he when he doesn't know what ya are to each other?"

I opened my lips, then shut them at the simplicity of his meaning when it struck right at the heart of the matter. Was Shaun scared of ruining our friendship? Was that why he'd never made a move?

You haven't made one either.

Strewth, can you give me a damn minute?

"Your octopus being chatty?"

"Is yours a pain in the butt?"

The grin aimed at me said it all, even before Dad nodded. "When I met ya mom, the damn thing wouldn't give me a minute's peace until I'd claimed her."

"It took ya a couple of months." I rolled my eyes skyward. "Imagine that for the last decade!" I groused, getting more laughter, which got my lips twitching seeing the funny side of it all.

"You have better control over ya shift 'cause of the time spent with Shaun. I spent a small fortune on clothes when my tentacles kept making an appearance and ripping through them to get to ya mom."

I choked back a moan of distress and held up my hand in defense. "Noooo, please don't. I do not need to think about you and Mom... just no. No. No."

His grin was unrepentant and I loved him for who he was. He'd made life easier than it could have been with being so different from my peers. He was the only other shifter I knew. It wasn't like there was some club we could join, or not that I'd found. I was different, same as Dad, and all the males in the family before him. An anomaly that came with the quirk of having a sea creature inside me. I'd adapted, but would Shaun?

That was the root of my worry. What if I revealed who I was and he didn't accept what I knew to be true in my heart—he belonged to me?

"He will accept ya. Fate knows what they are doing, son. Trust me." He kissed the top of my head when he rose. "Shaun loves ya. It's as clear as the nose on ya face. He just might need a little time to adjust when ya show him who ya are, is all."

The words ran around in my head, chased by the belief Dad held. I could feel the truth in his words. I stared at the sea and considered how I could show Shaun who I was without giving him a heart attack.

~/~/~/~

Showered and dressed in my usual swimmers, I strolled down the beach heading to Shaun's home, continuing to think about how to reveal my secret to him.

"Wait up," a familiar female voice called from behind me.

I groaned under my breath, slowing my pace, and glancing back at the jogging figure wearing running gear coming toward me.

Mandy and I had the kind of relationship siblings had. Very similar to her and Shaun, she sometimes tolerated me, other times she looked at me like a bug she wanted to squash. Something she was more than capable of doing. She was taller than me, something she'd—for a time—rubbed in my face when I'd stopped growing at fifteen and she and Shaun had continued to gain height. Shaun was a good five inches taller than her at six four.

"Whatsup gigantor?" I went with our teenage name for her, knowing it would piss her off.

An eye roll came as she came to a stop and reached for her watch, messing with it before she focused her attention on me. "You know you're showing a lack of maturity?" she said, the disdain coming with no hint of humor.

"Crack a smile. Come on, ya know it won't crack ya face." I couldn't resist putting my fingers at the corner of her lips and attempting to move them. "Ya might even get laid if ya smiled once in a while."

A twinkle sparked in her eyes, revealing amusement. She swiped at my hands. "You wanna get nakey with me?" She had a boyfriend. He owned The Rail, a popular restaurant bar in the middle of town. I shuddered for effect and a smile appeared that made me brace for what was coming next. "Or would you prefer that to be Shaun?"

"Shaun's my friend," I said, feeling heat creep into my cheeks when she gave a hearty laugh that drew the attention of two dudes who were coming out of the water. Her laughter, when she let loose, was at odds with her usual demeanor of 'back the fuck off'.

"We both know that's not all you want him to be." She poked one of her Christmas painted nails into my chest, stepping closer, seemingly oblivious to the stares of appreciation she was getting. "I've known you for how long?" Before I could respond, she carried on. "Too long, and I've seen the way you watch my brother, all hot lusting eyes."

"Hey, now that's bullshit," I spluttered, hating how I wanted to squirm under a stare that drilled into me as hard as her pointy nail. "We're best friends."

"Cut the bull crap. You've wanted to be more than friends for longer than I can remember." She got close enough I could smell the sweat coating her skin from her morning run. "I know why you haven't made a move, too."

Whatever heat had permeated my cheeks fled as ice ran through my veins at her knowing and sharing my secret. "What do ya mean?" I asked, working to keep the panic from my voice.

She didn't answer, instead she reached for my hand and tugged me towards the stairs leading up off the beach where it wasn't as busy. I went, albeit reluctantly, heart hammering hard enough my ears were buzzing when we came to a stop out of hearing distance from those on the beach. "Don't play stupid with me. The tentacles, I've seen them coming from your hands and feet. What are you?"

The buzzing increased and my eyes blurred. I bent forward, wrenching my hand from hers as I felt like I might pass out for the first time in my life.

A hand shoved between my shoulder blades, none to gently. "Sit down and put your head between your knees. Breathe."

My legs were happy to take a break as I dropped to my ass and did exactly what she suggested. Head between my knees, I kept my eyes shut, praying when I opened them this would all be a bad dream. Only the sounds and smells said this was no nightmare and Mandy had seen way more than she should have. It was pointless berating myself. The only positive, she wasn't freaking out, so that had to mean something. She also hadn't shared with Shaun... what did that mean?

"You finished having a freak out?" For the first time, she actually sounded like she cared.

I peeked up from under my eyelashes, trying to gauge if this was some sort of setup and she was trying to trip me up into confessing. "I don't—"

"Don't treat me like I'm stupid." She came and plonked herself next to me.

I stared at her like she'd lost her mind. Maybe she had? The fact she'd sat on the sand without a towel threw me. She hated the sand and never willingly sat on it. "Who are you? And what have you done with Mandy?"

She nudged my shoulder with hers and grinned. "There are many things I'd do for my brothers."

That knocked the wind right out of me. "Brothers?"

Another eye roll came with a frustrated expression that got her brows drawing together. "For an intelligent man, you sure can be thick at times."

Recalling what she meant by thick, I scowled at her. "Hey!"

"You have been a part of my family since you brought Shaun back to us when he got lost, and you know it. Why do you think I treat you the same as Shaun?"

I stared at her, a warmth growing in the center of my chest at the developing reality. Whatever she considered I was, it didn't change how she felt about me. It gave me hope her brother would be the same. Taking an enormous leap of faith, I uttered words I'd never said outside of my family. "I'm an octopus."

Nothing about her expression changed, absolutely nothing. I knew as I was studying her. "I wondered if it was that. I saw the tentacles years ago. It's cool. Can you show me?"

Was it really as simple as that? No dramatics, no hysteria, just a request to see what I look like. My mind raced with possibilities as the understanding dawned she'd known I was different for years. "On one condition."

"What's that?

"I need help to get Shaun out of the friendship zone and..."

"Yeah, you don't need to spell it out." A smile appeared, one I'd been wary of in the past. "Okay, but you have to listen and go with my suggestions."

I could do that.

I was a damn octopus and could juggle many things at one time.

How hard could it be?

Chapter Six

Shaun

Something felt seriously off with how Mandy kept grinning at me. She'd come back from her morning run later than normal and then parked herself in my line of vision, grinning like a mad woman. It was freaking me out. She never smiled at me like this—never.

"What's with you? You're staring." I'd made myself a healthy smoothie as an alternative to lunch to give me a boost. I brought the chilled glass to my lips, continuing to hold her gaze in an odd game of cat and mouse.

Her high ponytail bobbed as she moved her head in a motion that made no sense to me. "Just wondering when you're gonna grow a pair and confess to Fitch how you feel about him."

The mouthful of smoothie I was in the process of swallowing splattered the countertop between us. Green juice dripped off my chin as I gawped at her.

A sudden reality slammed into me, and everything inside me ceased at once. If she noticed I had feelings for Fitch, I was in serious trouble, because Fitch was way more observant than Mandy.

Wasn't he?

"I don't know what you mean," I hedged, keeping my voice steady, in the hopes she was just digging for info and was actually clueless. I placed my glass down when my hand started to shake.

"Please. We're twins and I've seen how you are around him. Those guys you dated—all of them—they look like Fitch. You have a type, and he is it!"

I had a type?

I wiped absentmindedly at my chin, a part of my brain aware it was still dripping green juice on the countertop. Did my ex-boyfriends all look like Fitch? I resisted the urge to take out my phone and scroll through the photos with Mandy looking way too smug for my liking. From memory, I ran through the men I'd dated and compared them to Fitch.

Smaller than me, wiry bodies, surfer dude looks, shaggy hair streaked with blond, which always looked like the wind had messed it up. Green eyes the color of the sea along the coast of Byron Bay...

My knees weakened and as I leaned against the counter to hold me up I scrabbled to recall how many of my boyfriends Fitch had the potential to see. Instagram being the place I shared shit on the most. Was this why Fitch had acted weird after the conversation about boyfriends? I'd not seen him this morning, and that was new. He'd normally be here, dragging my ass out of bed, regardless of how tired I was. There'd been no text, no call, nothing.

Pieces slotted together to form a picture, one I wasn't sure I'd purposefully avoided.

Shit the bed, I'd been dating copies of Fitch!

Had he noticed I'd been dating guys who looked like him and put two and two together and come up with four? Was he going to avoid me because I'd broached a subject that brought up the elephant in the room?

I ran my hands over my face and met Mandy's amused stare.

"You've just figuring it all out." Her tinkling laughter filled the quiet room as she came around the counter and slung her arm around my waist. "It's alright, I'm gonna help you get your... *man.*"

Alarm ran fast through me, making my shaking hands feel like I'd attached them to a fast moving jackhammer. "No! Whatever you're thinking, *no.*"

The determined set of her jaw showed she wasn't listening when she guided me to the large, overstuffed sofa I loved to lie on to watch TV. "Don't be silly. You evidently don't have the skills to catch a man as good looking as Fitch. Why else would you be going out with lookie likey rejects?"

"They were not rejects," I exclaimed, indignantly on their behalf.

"Yeah, whatever you say. So we need to think about date options that capture the imagination and show you are serious about Fitch."

How had I lost control of this situation? When had I admitted I was interested in Fitch in this conversation?

Those questions went unvoiced as she continued to steamroll over me. Twenty minutes later, I'd somehow booked a table at a restaurant that had a unique dining experience. One Mandy insisted would aid my sorry ass in talking about how I felt because we would eat in the dark. Allegedly, this would help avoid the difficulty of facing Fitch while I confessed I was interested in being more than friends.

Utterly bemused and terrified, I was at a complete loss to stop her when she took my phone and messaged Fitch to ask him out on a 'date'!

"You're seriously scary. You know that?" I croaked when the phone alerted me to say the message had gone. Could I pretend this was a prank if he rejected me?

"No, I'm the best sister in the world as I'm helping you," she supplied, just as my phone pinged. She looked down at the screen and my eyes closed, not wanting to see her reaction.

He's said no...

"What are you doing? Playing hide and seek? Aren't you too old for that?"

My eyes fired open, and I glared at her. "Isn't that what it will be like eating in the dark?" I took a steading breath and asked, "Did he laugh his socks off at the suggestion of a date with me?" The expression she wore gave me no hint as to whether her talking me into this had backfired.

"Don't you trust me?" Her pause was on purpose and my insides crawled to get out of me as I continued to glare at her. "Of course he said yes."

Unable to sit still, I bounced up, all my limbs seemingly working at odds with each other as I jerked this way and that while the shock of him saying yes worked through me. Was I really going to remove the barrier between friendship and more, despite the potential hazard of losing him? He'd been there nearly my whole life. The one I shared all my highs and lows with. He was my person.

"I can see the doubting Thomas' head appearing." She wore a look of sympathy as she got up and came to me. "Listen, you need to do something to show him you're interested before he decides to look for someone else."

The drop in my stomach at the very idea left me struggling to take a deep breath. It was like being on a boat that had just dipped and come back up on the wave way too fast for my body to acclimatize. "He might already have someone." I gasped, hating how bitter those words tasted on my tongue. "Have you thought about that in your grand scheming head?"

That was my fear, despite her saying he'd agreed. Could him wanting to go out with me just be a way for him to tell me he had someone? My antsy stomach formed into a hard knot that made me feel like puking as my mouth watered horribly.

"He wouldn't do that."

"How do you know?" I asked, staring her right in the eye, swallowing hard. "How?"

"'Cause Fitch is the kind of guy who brings back a lost boy and looks out for him. A guy who continually puts himself out to make sure he is free when his friend visits for a month every year without fail. Then spends all his time with that same boy, doing whatever the boy wants. I'd say that makes him more than your best friend, wouldn't you?" She patted me on my arm like I was stupid. "See? You do need my help."

Chapter Seven

Fitch

It was hard to keep my hands steady as I did up the buttons on the dress shirt I'd picked out. The green matched my eyes and it had short sleeves, leaving my arms free for what I had planned. I paired it with dark green shorts and slipped on a pair of brown shoes. They didn't feel right on my feet, and I considered if the restaurant would have an issue if I went with my thongs.

I stood debating as I finished dressing.

Mom's head came around the open door that led from the part of the house they'd converted to give me my own space. "Strewth, don't you scrub up well?"

Grinning at her and accepting the compliment, I bowed my head. "I swear ya'd think I didn't own decent clothes."

Her sweet laughter helped to lighten my anxiety at this whole situation. Listening to Mandy in the first place smacked of desperation. But I was desperate, so what could I say?

When I'd agreed, I'd figured it wouldn't be happening today, or that I'd only have eight hours to get used to the idea I was going on my first ever date with Shaun.

Mandy sure had worked her magic, which was great if I didn't feel like I might have a heart attack at the thought of revealing my secret. I was under threat of maiming if I didn't come clean to Shaun and tell him tonight what I was.

That being said, it had still been much more difficult to keep my distance from Shaun today, at Mandy's suggestion. She'd gone on about 'making him gag for it' but I'd not wanted to get into what she meant by that. Particularly as I was sure she'd not been talking about just my company and more about the sex stuff. What I'd also considered was that she might be worried I'd somehow blurt out the truth before getting the chance to ease him into a discussion around humans that could shift into animals.

If that wasn't bad enough, there was the whole 'I'm a virgin' thing. Had I told Mandy that? Had I fuck. Nowhere in any ocean was that something I was going to share with her. I was still working on processing our conversation from this morning, looking for the catch, convinced at any moment someone was going to say it was all a big prank.

A hand waved in front of my face and I blinked Mom's amused expression into focus. Shit, I'd zoned out. I gave an apologetic look. "Sorry, what did ya say?"

She reached and tugged on the collar of my shirt as if straightening it. "That ya have nothing to worry 'bout this evening. I'm sure Shaun is as nervous as you about taking this next step. Just remember, this is ya best friend. Ya soulmate, he will know that in a part of him."

"How did ya cope, really? Was it as simple as you and Dad say it was?" They'd always been honest with me. I couldn't have asked for better parents for being there when I'd had those difficult moments with coming to terms with who and what I was.

"I know ya dad thinks you'll have it harder 'cause you have been friends for so long, but I think differently on this. The connection I felt for ya dad knocked me sideways. I'd dated other men, but nothing prepared me for how I wanted to dive on ya dad and—"

"Mom!"

More laughter came as she tugged once more on my shirt, holding my stare. "It's life darling. We all have a past. Even ya parents."

"Not me!" I exclaimed.

She kissed my forehead, much like she'd done when I was a child. "You are a special boy who recognized the importance of ya bond with Shaun. Ya gave him room to live his life. Didn't push him to see you as more. I get why you did that, and it shows the merit of ya true character. Shaun will see that, too, when ya tell him about what and who you are."

"What? Once he gets over the shock that I manipulated him through Mandy and can turn into an octopus?" I muttered, not as convinced as she was about the ease of what was coming. I was pushing Shaun to see me as more than a friend, only he was under the misguided notion that he was the one taking the first step.

"You never mentioned Mandy was helping with this." Her lips quivered and her eyes gleamed with humor. "God help ya both."

"What's that supposed to mean?"

"Where are ya going tonight?" she asked instead, not replying to my question.

I shifted, not quite meeting her gaze. "To the Moonlight Grill and Wine Bar."

"Nice. That's the Japanese place, the one on Bay Lane, right?"

I nodded and stepped away to look back in the mirror, not wanting to add anything else to this conversation and let on that they did special evenings of erotic dining. She did not need to know that. "Yep, I went to have a look at the place earlier. It's got an all black interior with black marble tables that seat two people, and they all face the walls. Neat idea." I was waffling because of my nervousness.

"Yes, I know. Ya dad took me there last year for dinner... really great food. You'll love it with how much ya enjoy..." the pause was more noticeable this time, and I met eyes the same color as mine in the mirror and I groaned internally at the knowledge she knew what tonight was about. "Japanese cuisine." She held back laughter as she continued to look at me.

"Go away, you're bothering me and I need to finish getting ready or I'll be late collecting Shaun."

"We wouldn't want that, now. Not when you have got... *dinner plans*."

The innuendo didn't miss it's mark and I swung around, pointing to the door. "Out."

She held up her hands and grinned widely. "I'm going. Have a great night. I'll make sure our doors are closed to this side of the house." On that, she left the room and I heard the outer door shut as I shook my head, unable to help my grin at her antics.

I changed into my thongs, then went and grabbed my aftershave, slapping some cologne on my smooth cheeks. One more look in the mirror and I took a deep breath before heading out the door.

~/~/~/~

Air con on full, I'd shut the windows so I didn't melt in the December heat. Even at seven it was hot enough for me to regret my choice of clothing. The cotton felt too thick after wearing nothing but swimmers when I wasn't working. The engine idling, I honked the horn like I'd normally do, then second guessed myself right until Shaun appeared.

Holy smokes!

I'd made an effort for sure, but Shaun had knocked it out of the park. His shirt was white linen and the brief time in the sun had given him a rosy glow. Black linen shorts revealed thick thighs and muscular calves. I breathed a little easier at the black thongs on his feet. He'd styled his blond hair back off his face, allowing the square jaw to be more visible. His eyes crinkled with laughter as he swaggered towards me, holding something in his hand.

My gaze narrowed on the plain white box, then I reached over the seat to open the door, so he didn't have to linger outside in the heat. A masculine scent I'd never smelled before filled the cab as he shut the door.

"Hey," I said awkwardly, looking anywhere but at him at how uncomfortable the situation was.

Was I supposed to give him a kiss? Or was he supposed to kiss me as he'd asked me on the date? Fuck, this was complicated.

The tension crackled between us like it had last night when he'd asked about my dating history. Unsure how to break it, I sat there like a dag, uncertain of my moves. Not that I had any. I'd never been on a date before and I was coming to regret letting Mandy talk me into this with no experience.

"This is awkward," he muttered, shifting on the seat, the box getting shoved into my line of sight.

I sagged in relief that it wasn't just me and chuckled. "Yep." At his sigh, I chanced a look at him and the box he appeared to be waving at me. "What's in the box?"

The rosy glow coming from his cheeks went a deeper shade of red as the box got shoved into my hands. "Something for you. Take it," he growled.

Eyebrows raising, I took it and got a good sniff of his scent, which made me want to get closer to him. Only now, I was holding the box. I eyed the white lid suspiciously, bringing it closer. I sniffed at it, only getting Shaun's aftershave and maybe something sweet.

"Christ, I forgot how you are over gifts. Just open the damn thing before I reconsider and take it back."

The snappy tone broke the tension inside me. This was the Shaun I knew. The one who got impatient when I didn't dive into a gift and rip it open. For the first time since he'd got in the ute, I met his gaze and grinned cheekily. "Told ya, there's no fun diving in. Ya gotta treasure the moment." I sniffed at the box once more when I registered that the bottom of it was warm.

Heart beating fast, I flipped the lid and burst out laughing at the large, multicolored muffin sat in the box. Warmth flooded my chest at the sweet gift, one he'd evidently given a lot of thought to when there was no way he could have gotten this without pre-planning... and if that was the case, had Mandy's encouragement actually not been needed? Was he planning to ask me out?

The spike to my pulse made my hands tremble as I finally found my voice. "You went to Suffolk's bakery." The place had the best cakes in the whole of Byron Bay and was my ultimate favorite place to treat myself, only they sold out really early every day. When home, I usually helped Dad out with the early morning surfers wanting lessons so by the time I got there, they'd have nothing left.

"How is it still warm? And there's no way you were up that early to get there before they'd run out. Not your lazy ass," I pointed out, fishing for information.

His shrug came with him shifting his ass over the leather, making it creak due to its age, like the seat was too hot for him to sit still on it. He concentrated on the open box and mumbled, "Rang them to ask for a special delivery... for our date dessert... you know, later." Another shrug, this one a little jerkier as I watched his expression. He never got embarrassed! "You never eat two courses right after each other or not without a two-hour interval."

Fuck, he was too cute. The earlier idea of a kiss went from a maybe to a definite as I stared at the contents of the box. I closed the lid and twisted to face him. "Come here," I murmured, moving the box so it wouldn't get squished.

He moved slowly and I could see he'd clued in to what I wanted the second his large hand reached out, lingering over my neck, then around and into my hair. Warm fingers clasped the base of my neck and tugged gently until I met him over the central console. The heat of his body radiated out and drew me close enough for my chest to touch him as his lips hovered over mine. The wall of muscle beneath his linen shirt was solid and left me breathless.

"What?" His sexy, low timbre sent shivers through me.

Minty breath touched my lips as I willed myself not to think about this being the first time I was kissing a man and that this man was my soul mate.

Get on with it.

No pressure!

Then get on with it.

It was hard to push my octopus's thoughts out of my head when he wasn't receding. I closed my eyes and came forward the last few inches. Soft, was my first thought as our mouths touched. Then there was nothing, just sensations running wild and free.

The myriad left me stunned into immobility. My hands lay useless as his lips parted on a groan and I got lost in everything that was Shaun. Lost to the taste, touch, sounds he made as the fingers in my hair tightened and he changed the angle of his mouth. His tongue slipped over my lips, encouraging me to part them. When I did, it slipped into my mouth and he deepened the kiss on another moan.

The feel of his tongue sliding against mine brought a deep rumbling sound of delight to reverberate through me. My octopus lay utterly still in my mind, tentacles all on display. Every part of my body was alive with energy. In the water, in my octopus form, the warmth of it sliding over my tentacles and body was something that came with heightened awareness. Shaun's kiss was the same, only it thrilled, too. Drove spikes of desire through nerve endings, making my skin feel electrified, as if I'd caught hold of an electric eel.

The world slowed, narrowed down to the feel of his lips, tongue, fingers buried in my hair and his chest moving against mine. The scent of him, how he tasted to me. Sweet and sexy.

In the beginning I sat passively, allowing myself to sink into the much dreamed about moment. It was everything I'd hoped for, and I wanted more. As I went to reach for him, his mouth left mine and I groaned in complaint.

What was happening? Why was he stopping, didn't he like it?

I opened my eyes, trying to register what was going on.

"You taste of the sea," he murmured as he eased back, his chest heaving as he sucked in a breath.

I took in his appearance and became gratified to notice his eyes appeared unfocused, his face flushed, and his eyes were heavy-lidded, filled with the same need rushing through me. I couldn't find my tongue to reply because of how beautiful he was to me. How much I wanted to beg him to kiss me again and never stop.

Strong fingers stroked over the back of my neck, squeezed gently, then let go as he sat back into his seat. His hand dropped to his crotch, and he shook his head. "You better get us to where we need to go, or I might change my plans for this evening."

I bit my lip to stop myself from suggesting he do just that when I recalled what Mom had said about the driving need she'd felt. Sex—yeah, that would be great—only it wasn't happening before I'd told him what I was.

With a trembling hand, I turned the key, making the ignition grind with the fact the ute was still running. I blushed when he coughed, trying to conceal his laughter, and failed when he snorted loudly on the next bout.

I concentrated on reversing off the drive into the street and not getting us killed because I was horny and acting like a dag.

Heading toward the restaurant, two minutes in and I could feel the tension between us returning.

"What made you think to book this place?" I asked, searching for something to say, then realized my mistake when he tensed at the side of me.

Chapter Eight

Shaun

Still in the headspace of wanting to rip Fitch's clothes off and drive my aching dick into his body with as much vigor as I could muster, I tensed at the sound of his voice. Then at the question, when I wasn't in the habit of telling lies to my best friend. "Think Mom and Dad mentioned the place on a call. And I know you love Japanese food, so I thought it was a winner. You know, for a first... *date*."

I was gonna kill Mandy now I'd implied—when he realized what kind of night it was—that my parents got up to this shit too. Why did dating Fitch have to be so hard? Couldn't Mandy have just suggested going for a burger or something? Why did it have to be dining in the dark?

I continued to cringe internally at how this was going to look when I told him, because Mandy hadn't mentioned it in the message. And now we were at that point of no return without making it more awkward. I was stuck with figuring out how best to explain what came next. And right now, I couldn't think of a way that didn't come across as maybe a little creepy.

None of that took into account how much the kiss had affected me. I'd kissed a few guys over the years. Some had been better than others. One of my exes could turn my knees to jelly when he kissed me. Fitch... what could I say about the passive kiss he'd given me?

I resisted squeezing my hard flesh, leaking and trying to burst out past the zip on my linen shorts. The moment his lips parted and he'd allowed me to control the kiss, I'd worried for a few seconds that I'd come without so much as a stroke to my cock. The throbbing ache also hadn't eased after I'd—for sanity's sake—stopped. I'd never experienced a need to tear someone's clothes off their body and rut into them with no prep. Nope, I wasn't that guy.

Fitch? He drove barbs through my control, tore at it like it was a flimsy piece of cloth.

"Are you okay? You're lookin' a little tense, mate," Fitch asked hesitantly, the ute slowing down as I sensed him looking at me, drawing my attention to the fact I had one hand pressing down on my cock while I fisted the other at my side.

"I'm gonna be honest, that kiss kinda blew my mind."

The sound of the indicator was the only noise in the vehicle for a moment as he turned down a busy street, slowing for the traffic at the lights up ahead. "Is that a good thing?"

Was that nervousness in his voice? "Fitch, hasn't anyone said your kisses knock their damn socks off?"

Saying that aloud brought with it something irrational. A gut-twisting jealousy and violent urge to punch every guy that was lucky enough to have been on the receiving end of Fitch's attention. In hindsight, I was glad that Fitch had kept quiet the night before, with how I was hurtling from one set of emotions straight into another. It was much like the first time I'd tried roller blading and spent the first three hours trying to figure out how to get my limbs and mind to work together.

More silence as I twisted to watch him concentrate on the traffic as we crept into the heart of town. The places were as familiar as where I lived most of my life in London. Seeing a parking space up ahead, I pointed to the left. "Over there's a place to park that looks good and if I remember my directions, it's not far to walk."

He nodded, his jaw tight and his lips firming, continuing to say nothing.

My nerves danced with the tension between us. It wasn't something I liked as I wasn't used to it. When he turned off the engine, I looked directly at him as he sat unmoving with his hands on the steering wheel, looking out of the window, tension radiating off him.

"Do you wanna talk about this?" I asked softly.

When his gaze swung to me, I gasped at the rare vulnerability I could see. He didn't often display it, but with me he never hid. "I've never kissed anyone before."

I blinked slowly, going over what he'd said, then again as I licked at lips that still tasted of him.

Was he serious?

He sure as hell looked and sounded it.

But how could that be?

He was twenty-five years old!

"I... wow. How is that possible? I mean, look at you. You're gorgeous. Why would a guy not wanna kiss you?"

The sigh that followed was full of dejection and he looked away. His hands clasped the steering wheel. His lips moved, but nothing came out. Then his hands slammed on the wheel, and I jerked as he said, in an unrecognizable voice, "There's only ever been you. I never wanted to kiss anyone else, okay?"

If my heart could have rolled in my chest at the whack it received, I was sure it would have. I didn't need to see his full expression to know he wasn't messing with me.

Wow!

What else was there to say to that?

It was probably an ass thing to be happy that he'd not kissed or... "Are you a virgin!" I exclaimed loudly, as the thought struck me. I quickly wished I'd delivered the question with a bit more finesse at how he cringed away.

"Tell the whole fucking street, why don't ya? Maybe the people the next block over would like to know the status of my virginity," he snapped sarcastically, making me feel like scum.

"Shit, I'm sorry." I yanked on my styled hair and faced forward, sweat sticking my linen clothes to my back and ass while we sat baking in the ute. I opened the door, mind frantic on ways to make Fitch see I didn't see this as an issue.

"Sorry for being dickish." I picked up the cake box and gave him a grin, one that would normally get me forgiven. "To make it up to you, I'll even let you share half your muffin with me. What do you say?"

His lips twitched as he eyed me, then the box. "You bought it for me."

I shook my head, my smile widening. "Nope, I bought it for us. Didn't you see the size of it?"

His gaze dropped beyond the box, and I swallowed to wet my drying mouth at the sinful gleam in his eyes. "Not yet..."

My cock reacted and having wilted during the conversation, it perked right back up. "Come on, troublemaker. We'll be late for the reservation."

He hopped out of the cab as I shut my door and moved along the pavement, out of the stream of people, dressed and smelling like summer. He came round, locked my door, and nudged my shoulder, grinning. And just like that, we were back to being us.

I reached out for his hand and he stopped, making the guy behind him have to dodge to stop crashing into us. I raised a brow. "What? We're on a date. Hand holding is part of that," I explained, figuring if he'd never been kissed then there'd never been a date, either.

"Really? And where in the dating manual does it say that?" he quipped back, his voice thick with laughter as I interlinked our fingers and tugged him along beside me.

"It's in the Shaun 101 dating manual. I'll send you a copy so you can read up on that," I said with attitude, knowing it would get a rise out of him.

"Ya think we'll get beyond a first date? Cocky much." He exuded a happiness that showed he'd been holding back from me as he swaggered down the street.

"You're stuck with me." Weird thing was, that was exactly how I felt. Saying it aloud should have come out as a joke or had me freaking out. It wasn't any of those things. Him confessing that he'd never been interested in anyone else... I believed. Something we'd never done was lie to each other. His words were like I'd found a missing key to open something vitally important to me and it gave me instant pleasure.

"Mate, it's been the other way around since we met." His fingers tightened around mine as his brow furrowed and something about what he said struck a chord.

There was no time to examine the feeling as we arrived at the restaurant and I got slapped with a wet fish to the face by the reality of what was going to happen next.

"Hey, mate, why are ya trying to cut off the circulation to my digits?

I glanced down at our joint hands and blushed so hard, sweat gathered on my top lip as I eased off my grip. "Did you know they do something unique here for diners?" I offered instead, working to inject a jovialness I wasn't feeling now we were here. Doing anything but meet his stare, I reached to open the door.

The dimly lit entranceway gave some clues as I encouraged Fitch through the door first. A man dressed all in black gave us a polite smile. "Good evening. Do you have a reservation?"

"Yes, I've booked a table under the name of Mr. Gardner."

The guys' expression warmed. "A table for two, Sir?"

I nodded, recalling I'd had to order all the food and drinks when I'd booked. "Come this way, your server for this evening is Dani. She will direct your hands to where everything will be situated on the table." He glanced at the box I held with the muffin in. "Do you wish for me to take that?"

"Please. It's dessert, but we won't be eating it here."

The smile remained as he nodded and took the box before walking a few paces to a door. I held my breath when Fitch glanced from the guy to me. One brow quirked up and a light danced in his eyes that I couldn't fathom.

The door opened, bringing sounds and delicious smells and I glanced into the inky blackness, swallowing at just how dark it was inside. Sweat slid down my back despite the place being pleasantly controlled by air conditioning. "Enjoy your evening."

A woman who looked to be in her twenties appeared silently, also dressed fully in black, but had on some sort of headset that had to be night vision goggles. "This way, gentlemen."

Fitch's body brushed against mine. "Is this some kinky shit?" he whispered.

I chuckled. "Eating in the dark. Supposed to heighten the food's taste and allow us to talk freely without... you know..."

As he went to walk after our server, he stopped mid-step and glanced at me. "Ya forget to add getting..." he shimmied, his hips rolling suggestively.

"Get on with you." I shoved him forward into the darkness and muttered under my breath, "How the fuck are so bloody sexy and still a virgin?"

A choked laugh said I'd not been as quiet as I'd hoped but the server never broke from her professionalism. I suspected she'd seen, and possibly heard, it all.

I walked after Fitch, keeping my gaze away from the sexy ass swaying in front of me. Walking into the darkness, I kind of expected my eyes to adjust and I'd see something. Outlines, at least. I couldn't see anything once we were sitting and the door was shut. I imagined it was similar to what being entombed was like. I reached out and felt down the arm touching mine, feeling a little unnerved.

"Are ya freakin' out?" Fitch questioned, sounding curious and not in the least bit fazed.

"A little. I didn't expect complete blackness."

"It's all part of the experience," Dani said in hushed tones, somewhere off to my left. "Let me explain how this works."

Chapter Nine

Fitch

Whatever I'd expected of the evening, I hadn't figured it would be like swimming deep down in the ocean on the bed where no light penetrated. My octopus vision could adapt, and I considered it a cheat to use my animal spirit to enable me to see Shaun's reactions to everything. But he was so damn cute, getting all flustered and needing to hold my hand.

After Dani had directed us using a clock face for positions of things on the table in front of us, she left, which pleased me because her night vision goggles would see way more than I wanted her to for my big reveal. Although, how I was going to bring that up, I still hadn't sorted it out in my head. I'd already confessed to things I'd not planned on tonight. It seemed it was going to be an 'all out in the open' kind of night.

So far, Shaun hadn't done a runner and from the possessiveness he didn't hide at my confession to never being with anyone else, though mortifying, gave me hope. Hope that the next part of my big revelation wouldn't *suck*. Or maybe it would...

"That groan, was it for the sushi roll? If it wasn't, try it," Shaun said around a mouthful of food.

Had I groaned? "It's all delicious. If there's any left, ya wanna get it to go for your parents?" A choked cough followed, and I grinned at why. "I mean, maybe it will bring back memories of the last time they were here."

"Dude, would you stop!" There was a nudge to my bare knee. The hair on his skin rubbed against the smoothness of mine, igniting little fires.

I bit my lip to keep quiet as I shifted slightly closer, enjoying the freedom to touch and the fact that he couldn't see me or how hot and bothered he made me. A hand dropped to my thigh and heat sank through the fabric of my shorts as he stroked over the material. His pinky finger grazed my groin, causing my breath to hitch before moving away.

Was that on purpose? Fuck, I hoped so.

In my wallet I'd several packets of lube for later if things took a turn in a direction that led to nakedness.

"Sorry," I murmured breathlessly, willing the hand to come back.

Talk moved to friends we had in common and before long we were laughing at how Mandy's boyfriend Kev and one of my other friends had taken Bongo's Bingo, a concept that Shaun had talked about a few years ago that happened in England and brought it to Byron Bay.

"Oh my god, we have to go if Kev has organized one. When is it?" Shaun's excitement came with his body quivering against mine as he laughed. "We should rope in some of your friends. Serious man, it's fucking epic. Do you know who his special guest is?"

"I think it's tomorrow night. He only mentioned it in passing. He wanted to know if you were coming for the holidays this year."

There was the scrape of what sounded like glass on marble, but I couldn't see accurately what it was as I looked sideways at Shaun.

"Why wouldn't I have been coming this year? I've never missed a Christmas here with you." He sounded indignant, and I wasn't sure why.

"Probably thought with finishing uni and if ya got a job, they wouldn't have given ya time off."

The silence that followed came with a sense I was missing something when Shaun was motionless beside me. "I have a job."

This was the first I was hearing of it. I twisted more towards his seat, my knees pressing into his thigh. I really wanted to see him clearly and though my octopus had great vision, I couldn't quite catch the meaning behind the frown he was wearing. I reached up and pretended to miss him, just grazing his cheek with my fingertips before feeling along his jaw. "What job?"

His jaw flexed and worry gnawed at the pit of my stomach, tossing the food I'd eaten around. "I got a research job in Kemps Creek."

"Here, fuck." I brought my other hand up to hold his face bringing him towards me and, although he might have food in his mouth, I kissed him hard. I'd not wanted to contemplate his return to England again. It was the same every time he came, then left. I didn't dwell until he was gone.

"Why didn't you tell me?" I asked against his mouth, kissing him with way more enthusiasm at this new turn of events.

Only this time, his lips parted and I tasted the spices off the fish as his hands landed on my thighs and stroked upwards. The desire was stronger than with the first kiss and my octopus wanted in on the action. Before I could consider what he'd do, my hands shifted, and tentacles stroked over Shaun's face and neck.

I captured most of the scream in my mouth before Shaun tumbled backwards and brought me with him. Plates crashed and wood splintered as I landed on him with a thump. Air whooshed out of his chest and hit my face. A deafening silence followed before Shaun was pushing me off him to rise, his hands flailing around his body like he was brushing off a thousand fire ants.

Lights flashed on, and though they were low, I didn't miss the utter panic on Shaun's face as he looked at my hands, which had reformed. "What. Was. That?"

Each word came out like a bullet firing from a gun as he stepped back from me, his eyes glassy and his skin looking waxy under the lights. His hands rubbed over his cheeks repeatedly.

"I can explain," I pleaded. "Please, just not here, okay?"

The stilted nod was his only answer as I slowly got up off the floor, brushing off bits of food from my clothes, assessing the damage. "I'll pay for what we broke. Sorry," I said to Dani, who didn't appear to know what to do when she looked between us, wide-eyed with shock.

Had she seen my hands?

In twenty-one years, I had been super careful in public. *This is all your fault. If this ruins things, you are totally to blame. Ya hear me!*

My octopus stayed silent, which was probably a good thing with how scared I was feeling. My hands shook as I helped clean up, and then we went to pay the bill. Shaun couldn't get out of the place, or away from me, fast enough.

I watched him storm down the block toward the beach. I clutched the box Dani had returned to me and followed at a slower speed, trying to prepare for what was coming. I gave up, having never been in this position, so having no clue how things were going to pan out.

At the sandy path that led to the private section of beach towards my home, Shaun bent and took off his thongs, holding them in one hand.

The heat of the day had dissipated some, yet it was warm enough to appreciate the light breeze coming up off the water. Sounds of music, laughter and talking broke the quiet as the lights from the bars and restaurants we'd passed diminished as we stepped side by side onto the path leading down to the beach, not touching.

The moon was full and round, its glow making the sea appear black as I walked silently next to Shaun, waiting for him to say something. Say anything.

My thongs flapped against the sand, making a noise with each step I took. By the time we'd reached the far end of the beach, close to my home, my skin was crawling with nerves.

"Are you okay?" It was totally lame, but I didn't know how to start.

"Your hands were tentacles."

It wasn't a question, more of a statement, but I answered anyway. "Yes."

He swung to face me and I stopped, tilting my head back to meet his stare in the moonlight, assessing the level of anger. His eyes glittered and the jut of his jaw said I needed to tread carefully if I didn't want a smack in the mouth. "Those times in the water... were you touching me?"

I nodded, still unsure what to make of the flat delivery of the question.

"What... what are you?"

"A man—"

"Bullshit. I'm a man and I can't make tentacles appear out of my hands." He held them up, wiggling his fingers. A snigger caught in my throat at how he looked, making his hands dance.

"I am a man," I continued. "I just have an animal spirit, too."

"You're a fucking werewolf?"

He was back to screeching and this time I didn't hold back the laughter. "When have you ever seen a werewolf with tentacles?" I asked around the glee, still watchful of a fist flying at my face.

"It's not funny!" he exclaimed, then his shoulders shook before laughter burst out of him. The sound got whatever birds were in the trees to squawk and fly off. "Okay, that was dumb," he managed between bouts of raucous amusement.

"It was. But I'm not sure werewolves exist?" Honestly, I was clueless on that subject, so let it drop. "I'm an octopus."

That stopped the laughter. He wiped his damp eyes and stared at me intently. His gaze combed over every inch of me. "Inside you?"

"I suppose you could say that. I can shift parts or all of me into my animal form," I supplied helpfully, hoping it would help him accept me.

"Are you cognizant in that form?" This time there was definitely intrigue in his voice as he came closer.

This has to be good?

Why are you asking me? Answer him.

I rolled my eyes and answered, "Yes, though it can easily take over. Like it did tonight. I planned to tell you about it this evening, only when we kissed my octopus got a little impatient about getting his introduction." I gave him a sheepish smile. "He's been waiting a long time to meet ya."

Closer still, his hand ran down my arm, his fingers tracing over my muscles. "How long?"

The rumble of his voice sent sparks of desire down my spine as I stepped into him when he encouraged me closer. I tilted my head back to hold his stare.

"Twenty-one years," I murmured, then got onto my toes to reach up and kiss him. The box I held fell into the sand as I reached for him, my fingers sliding into the silky strands at the nape of his neck. His breath stuttered as I claimed his mouth in a hesitant kiss, unsure of how he'd react this time.

The worry seemed unfounded as desire sizzled between us. The hand touching my arm moved and it cupped my ass as the other wound around my waist. Effortlessly, he lifted me off the sand. My thongs thudded into the sand when I hooked my feet over his backside, wanting to get closer.

I captured his groan and swallowed it with the next moan when my hips rolled, rubbing my clothed dick against his. I could scent his arousal as shudders ran through him. I was aware of the gentle lapping of waves hitting the shore, voices in the distance, the feel of the air touching my bare flesh. Yet, it was a distant part of me. My main focus was on the man touching, tasting and making sounds that made nothing else matter.

On the next hip roll, his knees buckled and he tumbled onto the sand. I didn't for a second consider stopping. He perched me on to his thighs, a hand rucking up my shirt. His breathing was labored as his lips trailed down my throat. Open mouth kisses worked to undermine my control over my octopus, who was getting pushy, wanting to claim our man.

"We need to stop," I panted, struggling to get the words out.

"Why?" Shaun mumbled against my skin, sending a fresh wave of desire through me as he licked at the sensitive skin just above my collarbone.

Why indeed?

The tingling in my limbs gave me the answer. "My octopus," I gasped, as his fingers moved up the front of my shirt and touched my furrowed nipple. "He's likely to want to come out to play so he can claim you," I said, driven mindless as he was tweaking and pulling on my nipple and his other hand got to tracing the top of my buttocks.

I blinked to get my eyes to focus as Shaun's head popped up and his hands stopped moving. "Claim me? What's that mean?"

The lust was making it hard to get my brain to engage properly. "You're our soul mate. He wants to bite ya."

"Bite me!" he exclaimed, and I couldn't tell if it was fear or excitement that made his voice sound the way it did. Like he'd sucked on a helium balloon.

Cautiously, like I was treading on shells, I nodded, "Yes, bite you."

Should I bring up again the soul mate part which he'd seemed to have skipped right over?

"What's that entail? And do I need to bite you?" He eyed my exposed throat, where he'd somehow undone my buttons without me noticing.

"You can bite me too, but it isn't necessary." Not for the bond to take, that bit I left unsaid for now.

His gaze went to my mouth. "Do octopuses have teeth?"

"Nope. We have something called radulae, a bit tongue-like, in our mouths. But we do have beaks similar to birds. Cool right? They are at the base of our tentacles. They are great for cracking open the shells of clams and crabs. Mom did say it wasn't painful when Dad bit her to claim her."

Pleased I'd made it all sound sensible, I cried out as I landed on the sand when Shaun went slack jawed and appeared to lose all power in his limbs. He stared at me for long seconds as I realized I'd landed on my cake box. I huffed out a disgruntled sigh and rolled to the side, spraying sand everywhere. I got up and brushed off the cake crumbs that stuck to me, mourning the loss of my muffin as I waited for Shaun to get over his apparent shock about my parents. Where had he thought I'd come from?

Chapter Ten

Shaun

Punching my pillow, I rolled onto my back and flung the offending thing on the floor, staring up at the ceiling. My cock acted like a tent pole in the bed as I groaned at memories of how the night before had ended.

I ignored the knock on my door, too tired to people as I'd got no sleep. As much as I wanted to blame it on the jet lag, it was as much Fitch's fault, too. It was easy to recall the conversation that went down after he'd explained he was an octopus and it had fucking beaks. How many of the beaks would he want to use to bite me with? What did he mean by claiming me? Had he mentioned the word 'soulmate'?

As the questions kept coming, my mind whirred but my dick didn't consider all the thoughts in my head important when it was very clear about what it wanted—Fitch.

Until he'd brought up biting and his parents into the conversation, his kisses had hard wired my brain to shut off. Once I'd stepped away, the clouds of lust had lifted enough to consider that there needed to be more talking and less kissing. Problem was, at that point, I didn't trust myself to let the talking happen, so I'd made some feeble excuse about needing to think about what he'd told me and headed home, leaving him looking... hurt.

It had been a few months since my dick had seen any action besides my hand, and Fitch was a fucking temptation. His kisses... they put all my brain cells on the fritz, frazzled those fuckers until there was nothing inside me but need.

I thumped my throbbing cock when it couldn't see what the damn issue was. I pulled back the covers, tempted to tug one off when the door opened without ceremony. "Get the fuck out," I shouted, pulling the covers back over me and sitting up to hide my erection. "If you knock and I don't call 'come in', that means you aren't welcome!" I snapped, making sure Mandy got my point.

Clearly she was deaf as she ignored me and came into the room looking fresh as a damn daisy, sipping a smoothie from a straw. To make my point, I scowled at her and jabbed a finger at the still open door. "Out. Now."

"Someone didn't get any action last night, I see." She sat on the side of my king sized bed and gave me a pitying look, which she'd mastered at the age of ten.

She took another slurp from the straw and I ground my teeth together. I flopped back on the bed, hating the part of me that was tempted to open up to her, even as my cock wilted at her continued presence. At least there were some perks to her being in the room when nothing else had worked overnight.

I covered my tired eyes with my forearm. "If you've come to torture me, it's too late. I started the self-flagellation last night," I grumbled, hating that I continued to consider spilling my guts to her when she was to blame for this whole mess. "If I hadn't listened to you, things would've been fine."

"Oh yeah? Is that the thanks I get for helping you? You'd have been old and gray before you'd gotten up the courage to see what was right in front of your face. You love Fitch in more than the 'brother' sense and have done for a long time. Now stop this pitying act and fess up. How did you fuck up this time?"

I pulled the arm away from my eyes and met her stare with a hard one of my own. "How is it helping when... when..."

Oh fuck, am I supposed to keep Fitch's secret?

"Go away," I muttered crossly, bringing my arm back over my eyes, knowing she missed nothing. I didn't need the Spanish inquisition on my date. Not when it came with 'my boyfriend turns into an octopus'.

Is he my boyfriend?

My heart throbbed in the center of my chest at how he might dump my ass over the fact I'd run away. Also, we'd never really *had* the boyfriend talk. That was all in my head because I was the first guy he'd ever wanted to kiss.

"What did you do?" The question broke through my thoughts with an edge to it, which suggested whatever had gone on last night was all my fault.

She wasn't wrong. I'd handled things badly. But in my defense, it isn't every day I find out my best friend for over twenty years has kept a massive secret from me. "Nothing. I did absolutely nothing." Which, in part, was the truth, if I excluded the kissing and dry humping on the beach.

"Why do guys need to complicate things? I thought you'd have more insight as the person you're dating is the same sex?"

I lifted my arm, giving her a withering look as if she'd just said the stupidest thing in the entire world. "That's not the case, and I'm not getting into all that with you. I told you I don't want to talk about it." I heaved another sigh. "How can someone be something, then turn out to be something else?" I continued because I was too stupid to shut up. "He's... he's..."

"What? Perfect for you? Yes, I know this," she supplied, her lips never moving from the straw.

"Okay, that." I sat up, needing to move but not willing to get out of the bed when I was naked. I wasn't about to flash my junk at my sister. That would be gross. "I have... questions and it... is complicated... he's..."

"Can't you string the words together? You're giving me a headache trying to figure out this 'boy speak'. Just spit it out..." She grinned wickedly. "Or swallow, whatever works for you."

"Gross!" I scrubbed at my face, feeling the flush warming my cheeks at my sister even thinking about what I did with a bloke. "Listen, if you're gonna take things to gutter level, then leave."

She giggled, not looking at all repentant as she nodded. "Alright, I'll behave." I watched her try to rein in her amusement, shaking her shoulders and taking a couple of breaths as she put on a serious look. "So what happened? Talk me through the steps until it went pear-shaped."

The first part was simple. "He picked me up, I gave him the muffin—"

"Such a cute move, and I'm impressed you came up with that yourself," she said, interrupting me.

"Can't you just keep quiet for a damn minute and let me finish? And I have some experience of dating." I took a deep breath and narrowed my eyes at her in warning as I continued. "We chatted on the drive. He confessed to having never dated. We kissed and then we went and had dinner."

Her expectant look lasted a few seconds before she prompted, "And."

This was the tricky part. "He wasn't fazed by eating in the dark. That was more me. It was fun and more exciting than I expected." Right until my boyfriend's hands became tentacles. That part I kept to myself.

"You don't want me to interrupt, then you go quiet. And what happened next? There has to be more. You look like you found a penny after losing a hundred quid." An empty smoothie cup went onto my bedside cabinet and she twisted, bringing her knee up onto the bed to look more fully at me. "Seriously, you can talk to me."

I contemplated exactly that as I warred with myself and how to keep Fitch's secret. "Fitch is... unusual, and it brought up some questions which messed with my head. I left to figure them out before hurting him." I was proud I'd said something and not let on about Fitch being an octopus.

Her eyebrows disappeared under her fringe and my guts cramped when I figured immediately what part of what I'd said she was going to latch onto. "Unusual how?"

"It's hard to explain," I hedged.

She played with the hem of her shorts, keeping her gaze fixed on me. "You aren't giving me much to work with." She flicked her hair off her shoulder and made a face that said she was trying to suss out what she was missing. "When is he coming over today? What do you have planned?"

I shrugged, recalling how I'd left things. Normally, Fitch would have been here hours ago. The man was a morning person and loved to go for a swim...

My groin tingled at thoughts of him swimming in his other form and how he'd feel tangled around me.

Not weird at all when he had beaks at the end of his tentacles!

It didn't put off my dancing libido, even with my twin sitting right next to me.

It was a hard pass on doing anything to draw attention to myself. Instead, I ran through everything I'd read up on, in the middle of the night when I couldn't sleep, about octopuses. Who knew there were around three hundred different kinds? There'd been no mention of guys turning into them, though. No shock there.

She knocked my knee and tilted her head. "Wherever your thoughts went, keep that for Fitch. So, is he coming over?" She checked her smartwatch and frowned. "Oh, you really have pissed him off. You're defo going to need more help."

I held up my hands, trying to ward off any more suggestions. "I'll sort it on my own."

"How? He's not here dragging your sorry ass out of bed to go and do manly things all day so I'd say you need all of my help."

"Don't you have work… or something better to do?" I asked, trying desperately to come up with something that would sway her away from her look of determination.

The pat to my leg came with a wide, toothy grin. "You are the something better and I've worked solidly with the agency for six months so I can take some time off over the holidays. You aren't the only one who loves this time of year."

Regardless of the fact she was a pain in my ass, we'd had some fun times that didn't totally relegate her to the hateful sister pile. "What do you suggest I do? Besides eat crow and go apologize." Those seemed like the best ideas to me, as long as Fitch was willing to listen and, as of now, I wasn't sure he would.

"Have you ever watched '*Love Victor*' on the Disney Channel?"

Brow marred by frown lines, I shook my head. Where was she going with this? "Well, Victor's boyfriend, when he made Victor feel like he wasn't taking what he liked seriously, set out to prove he did in front of all his friends. We need to make sure it's something epic, so he knows you're utterly serious about 'eating crow' as you put it."

"Bongo's Bingo!" I exclaimed, recalling what Fitch had said the night before.

Mandy's grin matched mine and I could see we were on the same wavelength when she nodded. "You heard Kev is hosting a night at his bar, The Rails?" A furrow appeared between her brows. "The tickets, Kev said, sold like hot cakes."

"Shit, I never gave that a thought."

"Let me ring him and see what I can do. He likes me."

"Likes you?" I asked cautiously, unsure I wanted Mandy's brand of explaining what her boyfriend liking her meant. I'd once been stupid enough to question this and she went into graphic detail about how much a dude had liked her. Never again.

"Yep, in a non-platonic kind of way. The drop your knickers and shove you against the wall kind—"

I clamped my hand over her mouth. "I can't bleach my mind when you over share!"

"Spoilsport," she said against my palm. "I'll speak to Kev and get back to you."

Suspicion coiled deep inside me as I noted the glint in her eyes. But as Fitch wasn't here, I needed a reason to reach out... didn't I?

Chapter Eleven

Fitch

Once more I was sat on the beach staring at the water at a total loss on how to even begin to consider if I should go and have it out with Shaun. I groaned for about the tenth time.

"If you continue to make those groaning noises, people will think you're up to no good." Mandy's voice snapped me out of my head.

One glance at her smile and I shook my head. "Whatever ya have come to suggest, it's a hard no." A hard no that was as fucking hard as my dick. One that was unrelenting in expressing how much it wanted some action.

The taste of Shaun had set off a kind of chain reaction that left me in all kinds of pain, both mental and physical. Which I blamed on the smiling witch continuing to make her way to where I sat on the sand and had been for the last three hours, frying in the midday sun, too depressed to move and go into the water.

"What went wrong last night?" she questioned without preamble when she plonked herself down next to me, stretching out her tanned legs and crossing her ankles. Her thongs dropped to the sand, reminding me I'd forgotten to pick mine up after Shaun had practically run away from me.

"Everything," I exclaimed dramatically with an enormous sigh.

She nudged my shoulder in a friendly way I wasn't feeling. "It couldn't have been all bad you kissed each other."

I side-eyed her, knowing she had to have gotten that information from only one source—Shaun. "What else did he say?" Had he mentioned the tentacles?

"If you're wondering if he mentioned that you're an octopus then no, he hasn't said a word about that. I'm assuming that came up, which is why he's freaking out at home and you're acting all weird by not coming over to be with him." She rubbed the side of her face, staring at the sea. "How did he put it? You're unusual."

My lips twitched. Trust Shaun. A warmth that had nothing to do with the sun working on cremating me filled the center of my chest. "He freaked out," I stated. "We fell on the floor, broke some dishes and a chair in the restaurant when my other half decided that claiming him when we kissed was a good idea."

Her head moved so fast in my direction, her hair whipped out and hit my face. "Oh boy, no wonder he's freaking out!" She gave my arm a reassuring pat, a move that appeared to offer sympathy. It was hard to tell though with how her smile made my stomach dance unpleasantly. "Did you talk to him about it afterwards?"

It was hard to look at her when I squirmed at her directness. "Sort of. I told him I was an octopus, and that seemed to go alright... then..."

"Then?"

I ran a hand through my hair and went back to looking at the glimmering water, looking for answers. "I mentioned my octopus wanted to bite him, then explained in a little too much detail about the fact I had something that resembled beaks at the end of my tentacles." Her body shook and I glanced sideways, glaring at her. "Thanks for taking this seriously!"

"Come on, you have to see the funny side? And if you'd let me see what you look like, then maybe I could have helped a little more this morning when I found Shaun at home looking depressed."

There was some logic in what she said, I was sure, but the chance to change that was past so not worth dwelling on. "He didn't tell ya I was an octopus, so how were ya going to introduce that into the conversation?" Okay, I was going to dwell on it when I needed something else to focus on.

"I'd have gone with the mindless trivia he so loves... *not.*"

I chuckled at how she had in the past—many times—driven Shaun nuts with random facts that she somehow stored in that big brain of hers. She and Shaun were brainiacs.

"So, are you gonna let me help?" she asked after a few seconds.

What choice did I have? "What did you have in mind... this time?"

The smile morphing on her face suggested I should run, and fast. Did I? Evidently not, when I waited for her to answer me.

"Bongo's Bingo."

How Shaun had gotten excited the night before at the mention of it warmed me to the idea. "Go on."

~/~/~/~

I stared at Kev like he'd lost his goddamn mind when he held up the little red riding hood costume that clearly had not been meant for a guy. "What the fuck, mate?"

Deep brown eyes held way too much delight when I managed to shift my stare from the outfit he was holding out to me, to him. "I told Mandy, if ya wanted in on the action tonight, then you and Shaun needed to be helpers for my guy who runs the bingo. She said you agreed. It's too late to back out now. I told the original guys they weren't needed and they're busy now."

I had agreed to help... but not to this.

Fuck me sideways. "I just bet they're fucking busy! What is Shaun gonna think with me in this getup?" I cringed, heat flooding through me at the mortification of facing Shaun after last night, dressed as *little red riding hood.*

Kev didn't appear to be in the least bit concerned with the shrug he gave me. "He'll be wearing the other outfit. Little Bo Peep. It's got a bonnet... or that's what Mandy called it. Some weird English thing that goes on ya head." He shrugged. "So ya don't need to worry 'bout how ya gonna look."

I was going to kill Mandy with my bare hands.

I was!

Right after Shaun kicked my ass for believing this was me getting back at him. How else was he going to see it?

Before I could utter another word, I scented Shaun and my octopus, who hadn't been speaking to me, perked up. I spun around to watch him stroll through the bar, his expression wary as he eyed me from head to toe.

"There you are, Shaun. You two need to hurry and get changed. Things start in fifteen minutes." The outfit he'd offered me got shoved into my arms. It gave me something to clutch to and resist touching the man who was now wearing an alarmed expression when Kev picked up what must have been the bonnet he'd mentioned and a bag off the floor to shove them into

Shaun's hands. "Use the room off the back of the bar. You'll find Ronnie in there getting ready too, along with Jason."

He didn't hang around for the fallout, the coward!

"What the fuck is he talking about?" asked Shaun in a tone of voice that made it impossible to judge if he was annoyed or not.

"I... honestly... I... ya see... I..." my gaze dropped to the outfit I was holding, and I swallowed, marshaling my thoughts like tiny soldiers to get them in order. "We've been volunteered by Kev to help tonight, as the assistants for the Bongo's Bingo."

"You gotta be kidding me." Shaun glanced around the bar, which was already busy, and judging by the number of folks outside, was going to get much busier when things kicked off.

"Nope." The screechy helium voice had returned.

I held up my costume, working on trying to find the humor in the situation. "It'll be fun, right?" I could see myself grabbing a couple of cold ones before we started, as a peace offering, from the outraged expression Shaun now wore.

"You do not know what the assistants do?" he asked.

To date, I'd never been to one of these events, but Shaun had. I got a sense of foreboding that made the hair on the back of my neck lift. I considered if we'd need a bottle of the hard stuff to get through whatever was going to happen. "Nope. But how bad could it be?"

Those fateful words were like a black flag waving on the beach to warn surfers the water was dangerous. Those ripe tides were tugging me under the waves when I found out exactly how bad it could be when I attempted to squeeze my body into the tight, unforgiving lycra outfit in front of Shaun.

Mandy. Was. Going. To. Die.

Chapter Twelve

Shaun

I couldn't decide whether to laugh or cry at my current situation. The outfit I'd squeezed my big ass body into was a testament to Lycra's ability to stretch. The upper part of the dress was low cut and if I'd had full cleavage, everything would have been on show. Instead, my chest became squished enough to give me moobs. If that wasn't bad enough, the way the lower part of the silky dresses frills flicked out and sat right at crotch level, they showed off blue frilly knickers that grabbed hold of my cock and said 'hey everyone look here'. It was fucking mortifying.

I took another swig from the tequila bottle Fitch had swiped from the back of the bar as we'd been ushered through by Kev when he found out we hadn't moved. It was a fucking disaster waiting to happen with the alcohol swirling around my empty stomach and Fitch right there looking... hot in red and white satin.

For good measure I chugged back another big mouthful, feeling the alcohol burn the back of my throat but uncaring when things started to look a little hazy.

Hazy was good.

I'd been to Bongo's Bingo before and was well fucking aware of what the assistants did. The guy who'd stripped and used his wig to cover his cock while dancing in front of the crowd was on my phone. The video had gone viral.

"Maybe ya should lay off the tequila until the party gets going," Ronnie suggested. He was a massive guy with a buzz cut. He had a friendly smile and a quick wit from how he'd worked to put us both at ease when we'd entered the room to change. He was dressed like an 80's fashion reject with so much day glow on he was going to light up the night better than Sydney's New Year fireworks display.

"I will when I've blotted out the fact I'm wearing..." my hand swept down the side of the dress to the frills which I bounced, flashing my knickers at him, "this!"

"Ya look cute and good enough to eat," Ronnie said, with a smile that was all teeth and appreciation. Or I thought that was what I could see in his eyes as they roamed over me, but it was hard to tell with the tequila sloshing around my system.

"He's my boyfriend," Fitch stated in a possessive growl, moving to stand in front of me after snatching the bottle from my hand.

My cock stirred against the silk. "Hey, give that back," I slurred, swaying a little as I went to move around Fitch's back, not at all put out by the show of possessiveness with how things stood between us. Talking about shit was the last thing on my mind right then—kissing was more what came to mind—getting naked.

More tingly feelings ran down my cock, waking it further. Okay, maybe I needed to knock off the tequila for now. Going out into a mobbed bar flashing a hard-on would be... *fun*? I chuckled at the show everyone would get.

"On stage," said Ronnie through his laughter as I caught his gaze over Fitch's head.

"On stage?" I asked, confused. What had I missed?

Fitch patted me on the shoulder, wearing a look of concern, a deep furrow between his brows. He should look concerned we were about to perform an adult version of bingo, dressed for all kinds of mayhem. "Yeah, it's time to start."

"Great," I said, working on finding some enthusiasm.

Ronnie's laughter increased as the bastard went to the door leading into the bar. "Let's get this party started."

I grabbed the bottle of tequila and chugged it down. Cringing at the hit to my system, I coughed at the heat that hit the back of my throat and handed the bottle to Fitch. "I'd have a shot now! You are gonna need it."

Looking skeptical, he took it and swigged from the bottle, shuddered and then placed it on a table before he ushered me out of the door when chanting started. In the bar, the crowd made so much noise my ears rang, but the tequila gave me a nice cushion and layered over the panic at what was coming next.

Seeing no way out of the situation, and never one to back down from a challenge, or not when I was swimming in booze, I swayed my ass, frills flicking up and down as I squeezed through the crowd, feeling more than one hand touch my ass.

This was going to be *fun*. I grinned, the alcohol spreading through me at a rate of knots that made me chortle and get into the spirit of the game before I'd even reached the stage where Ronnie was now standing behind a set of decks. His hands danced in the air, encouraging the crowd to sing along. Unable to resist, I joined in, shimming up to the steps leading to the stage, my inhibitions left behind in the tequila bottle. Alcohol firmly in charge, I spun around and flicked my skirt up and shook my ass at everyone. I swayed a little as I spun back around and offered what I thought was a sexy wink.

I caught Fitch's wide-eyed stare and shouted loudly. "Are we ready to get crazy? Let me introduce my sidekick... Little Miss Red Riding Hood."

Laughter, catcalls, cries of 'yes' came with waving hands holding the bingo books and stampers. Fitch came up the steps... slowly.

Oh no, that wouldn't do.

I boogied my way over to him in classic 80's moves and pulled him onto the center of the stage, whispering in his ear. "This was your idea. Now let's see those moves, Red." I slapped his silky covered ass. "Make that tight ass dance for the crowd," I called out, over the noise.

The roar motivated me and I continued to play up to the crowd as Ronnie got to the serious business of explaining how the game worked and what the night's prizes were.

At some point, Kev brought us more drinks, which I happily downed because they made everything fun and Fitch laugh and rub his satin covered ass against my thigh, getting more rapturous calls from the crowd.

"Bingo," a guy called at the next round. As the music stopped playing, Fitch went into the crowd as I went to where the prizes were.

The evil grin that formed on Fitch's face made me laugh before he shouted out, "Up on the bench of shame, mate." The dark-haired guy, who looked wasted, got up and stood on the bench as Fitch directed. The crowd immediately started chanting 'You're a dickhead,' which made me fall about laughing.

Game back in play, music came with the call of some numbers, which aided in making people forget what the number was, leading to two more people having to stand on the bench before we got a winner. Looking at the prizes and the guy Fitch was standing next to, who looked straight to me, I picked up a double-ended dildo and waved it in the air as I danced through the crowd, more fondling happening.

When I reached the guy, he eyed what I held but didn't reach out to take it. "Mate, don't you want a good dicking?" I asked, giving those close to us a good laugh.

What I assumed was his girlfriend, the way she was hanging off him, snatched it out of my hand. "I do. Has been way too long!"

More laughter ensued as the music started again, and I grabbed Fitch and waltzed him back through the crowd, which parted to let us through. Or it could be I stood on several feet, and they didn't want bruised toes. It was a close call.

An hour later, dripping with sweat and loving every minute, I cheered with everyone when the special guest, who I'd not seen in the room we'd changed in like I'd expected, walked on stage. The Jason Kev had mentioned turned out to be Jason Donavan, and I giddily jumped about like I was his biggest fan.

When Jason stood in front of the decks and belted out a hit song, I tugged Fitch so the crowd could see us and danced with him, getting loud cheers. I swayed drunkenly with Fitch wrapped in my arms as Jason sang Especially For You. Only Kylie was missing, which kind of sucked.

But with Fitch plastered to my body, sweaty and sticky and smelling like all my favorite things rolled up together, the disappointment faded. The feel of his silky dress rubbing against my skin was doing a number on me. I mouthed at the skin on Fitch's neck. The need that had taken seed the day before became fueled by our closeness and enough alcohol to remove my inhibitions.

Stroking a hand down to his ass, I squeezed the pert flesh encased in damp silk and groaned against his neck. Fingers curled around the back of his neck to hold him still with need driving me, I crushed my lips to his and kissed him with every bit of passion swarming inside me.

Somewhere in my alcohol infused brain I got there was a crowd right there, but my need for him didn't care about the audience. This was Fitch, and I'd waited for what felt like a lifetime to have him cling to me like this. Touching me, kissing me.

"Get a room guys." Ronnie's booming voice came through the speaker behind us, and I stumbled backwards.

My lust hazed vision landed on the chanting crowd. "Strip. Strip, Strip."

Jason Donavon stood center stage, looking somewhat uncertain of what to do as music played, and the crowd ignored him in favor of what they wanted us to do.

For a brief second, I considered doing what they wanted until Fitch clung to me, his aroused dick not something I wanted to share with anyone. I held on to him, grinned at everyone and gave a bow before I dragged Fitch off the stage, hoping no one had noticed the hard-ons we were both sporting.

Outside, the air wasn't much cooler as I continued away from the noise of the bar, down a busy street, noticing then that people were staring.

Looking for a street sign, I struggled to recall which way it was to the beach with how floaty my head was. "Jonson Street. That leads to the beach, right?"

Fitch smiled dopily and plastered his body against mine. "If ya say so," he slurred.

Possibly as drunk as him, I tried to get him to walk with me. Halfway down Jonson street, getting further away from the crowded bars and restaurants, he clung on more like a monkey, making me carry his weight.

"Fuck, man." I glanced about, then wished I hadn't when things swayed, and I was sure I was standing still... possibly. "Climb on my back."

That didn't need a second invite. He moved and jumped at my back, knocking me forward as I worked to keep upright and cup his ass to hold him on me.

His laughter tickled my ear as his lips slid down the side of my neck.

Breathing became really difficult as my eyes crossed at how good his lips felt. My cock pushed against the damp, silky fabric and I staggered off down the street, looking for somewhere a little more private, completely forgetting our clothes were back at the bar, and what we were wearing.

Chapter Thirteen

Fitch

Shaun's scent tickled my nose, so I buried my face in the side of his neck, sucking in greedy gulps, wanting nothing more than to have his scent all over me. The hands cupping my ass burned the flesh beneath the silk, and I ground against Shaun's back, trying to get some much needed friction on my cock.

"Shit, stop it... or I'm gonna drop you on your ass," hissed Shaun, slurring just as much as I had.

I giggled, drunk enough to think everything was funny, as I squeezed my thighs tighter around his middle, rolling my erection up his back. Silk added to the overwhelming need to rut and get off, and spray come all over my soulmate.

Yeah, I really wanna do that.

The thought had barely registered before my jaw changed shape to clamp my mouth on the flesh of Shaun's throat, just as I scented how close we were to the sea. His groan rumbled right through him into me, and I bit. Tentacles formed around his neck as my senses swam at the first intoxicating taste of his blood in my mouth.

The world listed and I couldn't have said which way up we were as Shaun's body shuddered violently under mine. Fingers dug into my ass painfully, and though it registered, a part of me knew he didn't want me to stop. I could taste desire in his blood, his need to be mine.

Dad had said when I got my first taste of him, it would change me.

He was right.

Everything that made Shaun mine pulsed through me. Every cell in my body awoke to the joy of our soul's deep connection. It was as if I'd spent my entire life blind up to the point, but suddenly I could see the beauty of the world around me for the first time. Tears filled my eyes as I swallowed, biting a little truer, never wanting the moment to end.

Cum scented the air as my mouth carefully released Shaun's throat. I could smell it wasn't only me who'd come. Muscles loose, the wet, sticky mess in my underwear hadn't dampened the desire still looking for a target to unleash itself on.

Tentacles stroked lovingly down the front of Shaun's dress.

"Fuck," Shaun gasped before his hands loosened and I slipped a little before he tightened his grip once more. Then air whistled past my face as I blinked, trying to get my brain to work out how. Only there came an overwhelming sense of panic at what my liquor-fueled brain had just done in public.

It's dark.

It's okay.

No one saw.

Had they?

Deep in my panic, it took several seconds to register that I was shaking, only not from what had happened but by being jiggled about by Shaun, who was somehow... *running.*

A stupid grin spread over my face, the panic receding. "You is so fucking macho. It's hot!" I exclaimed and got a breathless curse in response. I buried my face back in his neck and licked at the mark I'd made. "So's ya ass in them knickers."

A violent shiver ran through Shaun, nearly turfing me off him as he cursed once more. "I'm gonna kick your ass for this."

"Can that wait until after you fuck it?" I murmured, not at all worried. Shaun would never hurt me.

The groaning noises Shaun made sounded painful, so I kept my other thoughts to myself, waiting until he decided he was happy with wherever he was taking us. My eyelids drifted shut and I snuggled in, letting the movement lull me. I'd never been so fucking happy.

~/~/~/~

The tongue glued to the roof of my mouth tasted like I'd eaten a whole garbage bag of shit. As that registered, so did several other things. A pounding in my skull, the need to pee, and that I felt like I'd drunk the entire ocean. None of that got my pulse tripping over itself, though. No, that was the feel of a very large, warm body plastered to mine. The weight of a thigh pinning my legs to the bed came with another reality. I was still wearing...

I peeled open one gritty eye and somehow got my head off the pillow to look down.

Fuck!

How did we get back to mine?

Had I...

My eye shut, and I groaned, swallowed, then regretted it with the awful taste in my mouth. My thoughts jumped about so fast, it was like I'd overdosed on an energy drink that always made me feel like my heart was going to burst from my body. The need to pee took a back seat when I worked to run through what I could remember of the night before.

Flashes came with increasing speed and I winced at how I'd be the talk of Byron with some of my antics, and how Shaun had encouraged me. That outfit he'd worn should have come with a warning of 'it takes sane guys and turns them into a horn dog'.

He's our soul mate.

The smugness registered past the pounding and both eyes popped open. "You bit him!" I exclaimed and Shaun's heavy thigh shifted higher and crushed my... morning wood. He made a snuffling noise before the arm lying over my middle tightened to pull me closer to him.

Fuck!

Fuck!

Fuck!

The chanting continued as I carefully lifted my free arm and moved the hair away from the side on Shaun's neck, needing confirmation we'd bitten him.

My groan had fuck all to do with the awfulness that was my mouth, or the pounding jackhammer in my head. No, it was to the mark at the junction of Shaun's neck where it met his shoulder. Words floated through my head. *"I'm gonna kick your ass for this."*

What have you done?

What we did.

I hated my octopus. I really did.

"Whatsup?" Shaun mumbled, his warm breath touching the skin on my throat and sending sparks straight to my dick, which throbbed with a renewed vigor that made the urge to pee intensify.

"How are ya feeling?" I hedged when his head lifted and his sleepy eyes met my panicked haze.

His thigh shifted a little higher and brought attention to the erection poking my side. "Hard."

He was playing with me.

That had to be good?

"Nothing else?" I persisted, desperately wanting him to acknowledge what I'd done.

What we did.

Stop splitting hairs, will you!

He came up to sitting so fast, the mattress dipped and I got a rush that made my mouth water in that horrible, want to vomit way. I eyed him with caution. Was this the ass kicking bit of the morning?

He rubbed at his skull, eyes wide, staring at me. "You're talking in my head," he exclaimed. "How? And why am I splitting hairs?" he asked, looking completely baffled.

It's our connection.

He scrubbed his hands over his face, then looked at me. "Okay, I need coffee. Lots of it if I'm gonna deal with whatever is going on here."

He rolled off the bed and stood, his cock standing proudly from his body and making it impossible to get me to think about anything other than how mouthwatering it looked. Long, thick, and veiny, I wanted to see if it tasted as good as it looked.

"Eyes up here," Shaun muttered, sounding more amused than pissed. He tapped at his chest and that wasn't helping me any with the width of his broad shoulders or how he had a trail of silky looking hair leading straight to his cock.

"That isn't any better, can I just say. You are fucking naked and looking more glorious than any sunrise or sunset I've ever seen. And if that wasn't enough, I can still feel where ya plastered yourself against me, mate."

He gave an evil chuckle, one that worked its way down to my cock and lodged in my balls. Off the bed like a professional soccer player chasing the ball, I ran to the bathroom. I slammed the door, my trembling fingers locking it behind me for good measure as I shouted, "Asshole!"

Breathing hard, I went to the toilet and peeled off the cum encrusted knickers, cursing loudly when it tugged on my skin unpleasantly. Legs parted, I stared at my cock, hoping it would figure out how to pee with how turned on I was as the pain in my bladder worked up another notch.

I refused to acknowledge that Shaun was on the other side of the door, laughing his ass off at me. One look in the mirror and I didn't need to figure out what had caused the laughter. I looked like one of the ugly sisters in Cinderella, squashed in an outfit two sizes too small and thinking I looked way hotter than I actually did in the light of day, with no tequila to blur my reality.

Mandy is going to die... slowly!

Very fucking slowly!

Chapter Fourteen

Shaun

Staring at the locked bathroom door, I worked to get my laughter under control. After Fitch had fallen into a drunken sleep, I'd debated what to do next. The beach was deserted because of the lateness of the hour, so I'd perched on a wall with Fitch on my back and gained my breath, and some of my brain cells, back. The exercise had worked off some of the effects of the tequila, which had buzzed through me like when I'd once taken hydrocodone when I'd hurt my back playing rugby. I'd been off my tits and the feeling I'd had wasn't dissimilar.

Was that natural high Fitch?

Last night I'd given it little thought. Sticky from running, cum coating my knickers from his bite, I'd few options to me. Against my better judgment, I'd given in, realizing I couldn't sit dressed as we were on the wall all night. Fitch wasn't overly heavy, but holding him up for five hours hadn't been appealing. That I'd shoved my phone into the front of my dress allowed me to call the person responsible for what had happened. Mandy.

She had been at The Rail's. I'd seen her laughing her ass off. I'd no qualms about waking her so she could get her ass out of Kev's bed.

The fun had begun when she'd arrived, and I'd realized the error of my ways with how much I hated riding shotgun with her.

That I smelled of cum hadn't entered the equation. Fitch hadn't so much as stirred as I'd placed him inside the vehicle or when we'd arrived at his house after listening to Mandy rag on my ass.

Using the hidey key, I let us into the part of the house Fitch's parents had converted for him so he had his own space. Mandy, through her laughter, had held doors, enabling me to carry Fitch to his bedroom. She'd left with my promise of retribution as she's snapped a damn picture of us.

I'd stripped, cleaned myself, brushed my teeth and drank a gallon of water, all the while ignoring the raging hard-on from the sleeping man in the bedroom.

My hand unconsciously went to my neck where Fitch had bitten me last night. I stared at the mark at the base of my neck. The second I touched it, a fresh wave of desire surged through me, and I panted as wild urges came from my fingers running over the supersensitive, puckered skin that felt like something directly connected it to my cock.

Before I could register my intent, with the fresh need firmly taking charge, I got up to pound on the bathroom door. "Open up, now," I demanded, with my teeth aching in my jaw. The memory of how this wasn't the first time it had happened came with another thought.

Is this my need to claim Fitch? Bite him?

When that idea didn't repulse me, I hammered on the door, wanting...

What has he done to me?

Whatever it was, it left my patience to get to him somewhere back on the beach. There was the sound of a toilet flushing, then water sloshing as I stood and waited, not so patiently, as I moved from one foot to another, eyeing the door and considering how hard it would be to kick it in.

As I was about to test the theory, the sound of the lock clicking had me reaching for the handle and shoving it open. It was as if I'd reached an unfathomable level of desperation to see Fitch, to touch him, to bite him.

Nothing made sense as I charged into the bathroom, noting he was still in the dress, but minus the pants. I grabbed hold of him and groaned at the simple touch, easing the tightness in my chest as I lifted him clear off the floor.

"Wrap your legs around me," I growled, desperation making my pitch low and gravelly.

Wide eyed, he did as I asked, his erection poking up under the hem of the dress as I spun and went back to the bedroom. He didn't have time to bounce on the bed as I dropped him, his legs splayed open as I lunged for him, tearing at the lycra.

Anything in my way of touching Fitch was a barrier I wasn't in the mood to tolerate, or take the time to remove it carefully. I shredded the dress. The violence of the need would have been shocking if I'd had the ability to stop and consider my actions. Only the sleeves held the dress on him as I feasted on his tanned chest that was heaving as he whined and moaned, his leaking cock leaving a trail over my stomach as he thrust up against me.

"Bite me," he begged breathlessly. "Bite me. Fuck, pleaseeeee."

His movements were as erratic as mine as my teeth felt like they were attempting to push out of my jawbone. I sucked a furrowed, brown disk into my mouth, nipping at it and getting a needy moan in response. The sounds, adding to the overall swirl of my emotions, removed all common sense. Never one to let my desire make me careless with a lover, Fitch pushed at those boundaries with a battering ram. I could feel it removing any finesse I might have had as my hands roamed over his body, frantically trying to memorize every inch of him. The smoothness of his skin was silkier than the dress he'd been wearing. The freedom to touch, to taste what belonged to me was like I was drunk once more. Only this time on the taste of Fitch. I never wanted to be sober again if it felt like this.

My shaking fingers glided over firm ridges of muscle as I bit hard on his nipple, tasting the merest hint of blood on my tongue as I lapped away the sting. Chili heat, the kind that blows tastebuds to hell and back came as I swallowed, wanting more.

"So good," Fitch gasped, fingers clutching my head, his nails digging into my scalp as he writhed under me.

"You're so fucking beautiful," I murmured as I looked at him, flushed, aroused, and smelling like the sea and uniquely Fitch. "I want you so bad. Fuck, I'm shaking."

I sucked in a breath that didn't help when the hooded eyed, sexy fucker beneath me let go of my hair to play with both his nipples as if he was strumming a damn guitar. He tugged hard enough to stretch the skin as he offered them for me to take a taste.

My erection, which was so fucking hard and painful, jerked in time to the fast beat of my pulse. Pre-come ran down the length onto Fitch in a stream, his skin glistening with my cum.

"I didn't realize what a fucking tease you were," I rasped as I came forward to lick the tip of one, then the other bud he offered. "You like nipple play?"

"I do. Only it's much fucking better when it's with you." His voice sounded rough and broken at the confession.

I bit down on the tip, getting a keening sound in response. Each noise that poured from his lips added fuel to the raging fire, wanting to break free and burn us both. I licked and teased. The salty taste of his skin was addictive as fuck. His hand moved back to tug at my hair, working to stop me from pulling away. "More... fuck yeah."

He shifted his legs, and they wrapped around my hips. He crossed his feet over my ass and pulled me in closer to him until there was no space between us. I rocked my slicked dick up against his. Skin on skin, it built the fire to an inferno of flames as the ache in my jaw became impossible to ignore and, running on pure instinct, my teeth sank deeper into Fitch's flesh, close to his heart.

He howled like a werewolf, and I chuckled, not at all grossed out that I had a mouth of coppery blood. It was part of Fitch, and I wanted any part of him in me, on me, anyway I could get him. If it wasn't logical, who the fuck cared?

The whining and needy whimpers were all I could focus on as I swallowed deep. Bold and wild, he writhed under me, moaning his pleasure for all to hear.

He was mine.

Mine!

Yes, yours, only yours.

At the words rocking around my brain, his cock spurted over mine at the next glide of my hips. It triggered my release. Muscles straining, the world blurred. Sweat dripped from my hairline as my hips moved erratically. I rode the waves of pleasure like a pro surfer as Fitch clung to me and panted as hard and fast as I was.

Seconds, possibly minutes later, I squished Fitch into the mattress as I collapsed against him, exhausted and limper than a noodle.

"Mate, ya squishing me," he mumbled next to my ear.

I grunted. It was the best I could do.

Instead of his hands pushing me off, they came around me and held me closer. His breathing slowed and the heart jumping hard enough it matched mine, settled as the sweat cooled on my skin.

High as a damn kite, I drifted on the euphoric feelings.

A hand trailed down my back, running over the base of my spine, tickling the crease of my ass before moving back up. Fingertips glided gently over my skin and I groaned. I'd always loved someone running their hands over me. The fingertips lifted and I was about to complain but then there was the barest of touches coming from... *tentacles.*

Memories of last night after Fitch had bitten me came flooding back at how his tentacles had run over my throat, over my bite mark, giving me an erection so fast after I'd come, I'd lost the ability to figure shit out with the lack of blood in my head. The one that hadn't come back online until I'd reached the beach, wanting to be alone and somewhere private.

Breathing out, I lay as I was, sensing through the odd connection I had with Fitch that he was testing the waters. Maybe the depth of my freak out, of which I'd had many in the past—with what I knew now, was him trying to tell me in his own way what he was. And that brought back a flash of a memory and I lifted my head to look sideways at the hooded gaze, which held hints of fear.

It was there between us. "I hurt you, didn't I?" His brow furrowed in confusion. "When we were fifteen, and you tried to show me what you were, and I freaked out... and said..."

"That there are all kinds of weird shit in the sea, like octopuses. That you thought those things were creepy with all their suckers and tentacles. Yes, I remember."

The flat delivery sent shards of pain through me. It was both great and difficult to read him so clearly. Great, because there could be no miscommunication. That also meant I got all the pain I'd caused, too. Something I'd never have knowingly done to him.

I traced a finger down the side of a face that was as familiar to me as my own. "I'm sorry. I can't go back and kick my stupid, dorky self's ass. I would if I could..." Pausing, I inhaled his scent, needing it to ask what was there at the forefront of my mind. "That reaction stopped you telling me about us, about what we could have together, didn't it?"

His nod added a hammer blow to my heart, making it beat faster as we stared at each other, and I released a shuddery breath. It was there, the love I'd chosen to ignore... or more not know what to do with when it could change what was between us. I'd always known our friendship was special, just not the full extent of how special.

Neck straining at the awkward angle, which wasn't great for having this kind of serious conversation, I rolled and brought him with me, not wanting to let him go. I shuffled my ass up the mattress until I could rest my head on the back of the bed. I noticed he still had the torn dress hanging on his arms.

Happy I'd gotten us both more comfortable, I helped take off the dress and threw it on the floor. I threaded my arms under his armpits as his forearms came to rest on my chest. Then he placed his chin in his fists, staring up at me, waiting.

"I was scared of changing things between us." As I said it, I knew it was the absolute truth. "I got what we had was special. The friendships I had with others didn't have..."

"A soul connection," he supplied, in total seriousness.

"I suppose now I've bitten you, I'd say that about sums it up."

His eyes crinkled at the edges and his lips slowly lifted into a smile that had the ability to make a shitty day feel so much better. My whole life he'd been there, being Fitch. Waiting for me to see him.

I'm such a fuckhead!

Maybe...

It was going to take a bit of getting used to, hearing him in my head, but I chuckled at the smirk he aimed at me.

"Why did ya bite me? Not that I'm complaining," he added quickly, at the quirk of my eyebrow.

"I can't say why for sure, I just had this ache in my teeth and jaw that I knew would only feel okay if I bit you." I shrugged, not at all happy with how I'd explained myself. "There was a wildness to the feelings going through me." I blushed as I confessed, "I wanted to have a part of you inside me."

His cock thickened against the thigh it was lying against and his smile morphed into a giant grin. "I'm happy to have any part of me... *in ya.*"

I chuckled at his waggling brows and the wicked glint in his eyes. "Is that right?" My thoughts went straight for the gutter.

In the process of rolling us over, wanting to feel another part of him inside me, there was a loud knocking on Fitch's outer door. We both glanced towards the open bedroom door and groaned in unison. "Do you think if we ignore it, your parents will go away?"

He shook his head, his nose wrinkling as he sniffed the air. "It ain't my parents," he said, rolling his eyes. "It's Mandy."

I groaned, sitting up and letting go of Fitch, which was the last thing I wanted to do. But knowing my sister as I did, she'd not go away until we'd answered her. And if we didn't she'd only keep banging on the door or worse, go get Fitch's parents to let her in on some ruse. She was cagey like that.

I looked about the room for my clothes, then groaned anew at where I'd left them last night. "You got a pair of shorts I can use?"

His laughter was rich as he eyed my lower body. "They might fit one ass cheek, if ya lucky."

I rolled my eyes, about to step back to the bed, when the next round of knocking came louder than the last. "Then you get dressed and go answer her. Tell her I left."

He got off the bed. Gloriously naked and aroused, he swaggered towards me, the light creeping past the blinds casting shadows over his muscle definition. He did not get dressed. Instead, he came to a stop in front of me.

My gaze shifted from his knowing smirk to the bite mark on his chest. The flesh didn't look like it should as I became fixated on the healing skin. "How does it look like that?" I pointed and drew his gaze to his chest.

"It's the same as yours."

My hand rose to touch the mark, and what I'd not registered the night before when I'd looked at myself in the mirror. "How?" I asked, flabbergasted at the speed of healing. Was this an octopus thing? Was I now part octopus?

"No, ya not part octopus," he said around the laughter he didn't hold back. "Not in the way you are thinkin'," he said, answering my unspoken question as the next round of hammering hit.

"Put something on and go get rid of her before she goes to get your parents."

Given the smell of cum and sweat, along with the state of the bedroom, it wouldn't take much to figure out what we'd been up to.

Finally, he grabbed a pair of shorts and slipped them on as he went to the door. With my head a jumble of questions, I realized too late that he'd not covered his chest.

"Put on a T-shirt," I hissed, dashing after him as he tugged open the door to reveal an overly amused looking Mandy.

She glanced from Fitch to me. Her gaze dropped and I stepped back to slam the bedroom door on her laughter. Heat warmed my cheeks as I scanned the room looking for something, anything to cover my body, knowing it was too late to lie now she'd seen me... naked!

I buried my head in my hands and willed the embarrassed heat away. *Why couldn't I have gotten a brother?*

Stop having a meltdown and get out here. I'm not facing her alone. Fitch's voice in my head caused a wide, silly grin to spread over my face.

You're my soulmate!

Yep, now hurry the fuck up!

Chapter Fifteen

Fitch

It was hard to be pissed at Mandy when she'd helped to bring about what had happened this morning. I just wished she'd stop eyeing my chest like I was an insect under a microscope.

Can you hurry and bring me a T-shirt?

You literally have nothing that fits me!

I can't help that.

There were some mumbled curses, and I looked at the bedroom door, wondering what the hell he was doing in there.

"You gonna offer a girl a drink, or do I need to die of thirst?" Mandy walked past me, hand not carrying a bag, slapping my ass, her nose wrinkling. "You might want to have a shower."

I groaned and kept some distance between us, now feeling the crusted cum on my skin. I'd barely had time in the bathroom to rinse my mouth out with water. "It's not my fault ya rocked up here, hammerin' on the door to get in." I pointed back to the door, not that she noticed as she was at the counter filling the coffee maker. "Ya can always go back out the way ya came."

"Why would I do that when I went to the effort of bringing back your clothes?"

"Ya have Shaun's things with ya?"

Tinkling laughter filled the room and she glanced over her shoulder, her hair swinging. "Kev wants the outfits back so I thought I'd kill two birds with one stone." Her gaze dropped to my chest, distracting me from what she was saying.

"Ya wanted to see if we'd..." I found my face warming when she nodded and didn't pretend to not understand where I was going with the conversation before I hauled my ass back from the brink of an over share.

"Is that bite mark from Shaun?" she continued, when I shut up.

Bubbling and hissing came from the coffee maker while she turned her full attention to me. My face felt like I'd sat it over the steam of the coffee maker, the way the sweat gathered on my top lip.

"Nope, not talkin' 'bout that." I went and picked up the bag she'd dropped on the floor by the counter.

As I walked back to the bedroom door, I felt her eyes on me. I slipped through the door and shut it firmly on her. I glanced at the empty room, grinning at the freshly made bed and pile of bed linen poking out of the hamper in the corner of the room.

Shaun was a neat freak.

I followed the sound of running water and stepped into a steam-clouded bathroom. The tall figure behind the wet glass left little to my imagination and the arousal that hadn't fully dissipated—and I wasn't sure would ever with the connection we now had—flared fully to life.

A groan came as he popped out from behind the glass, dripping onto the tiles. He shook his head, pointing to the door. "Out. My sister is in the other room."

"What?" I asked all innocently.

"Don't 'what' me. I can feel your intentions to get in here with me and…"

I filled his head with all the wicked thoughts that ran through my mind. Each dirtier than the next and all of them ending with me doing something fun with my tentacles and his cock.

A flush crept up his neck and highlighted my bite mark. The scent of his arousal flooded my nose as I took a step towards the shower.

He held up both hands, warding me off. Desperation rolled off him and made my cock bounce at what he wanted as badly as me. "I swear, if you get any closer, I… I'll not be responsible for what my sister sees when she comes barging in through the unlocked door," he ground out through clenched teeth, a look of daring on his face I was more than happy to accept.

"If you two get in that shower…" Mandy called from inside my bedroom. I darted for the bathroom door, which I'd left open, to slam it shut on her laughing face before she could continue.

I looked at Shaun, wanting some reassurance she'd not spy on us. "She wouldn't, would she?"

"This is Mandy. Who the hell knows if she'd cross that boundary?" he supplied, sounding way too skeptical about what Mandy would or wouldn't do, making my cock wilt at thoughts of her seeing me and Shaun together.

I dropped the bag I was still clutching on the sink unit. "Ya clothes are in here." I kept my gaze averted and went back to the door, opening it to peek out. Mandy was nowhere to be seen, but I didn't trust that she wouldn't come back.

Shaun grunted and his laughter came out sounding choked. "See what she wants. I'll be out in five."

"Why do I have to go face her? She's your sister," I muttered crossly, finding no amusement now I'd been cock blocked.

"And yours," he pointed out before I shut him in the bathroom, only to grin at the truth.

"Hurry, I'm getting bored out here." Her shout got me grabbing the first top I could find and slipping it on before heading to get some of the coffee I could scent in the other room.

"Why do ya have to be so damn nosy?" I asked while I poured both me and Shaun a drink, fixing his coffee the way he liked. The hunger in the pit of my stomach made itself known, so I grabbed two raisin bagels and some cream cheese.

Silence, so unlike Mandy, got me twisting to see her watching me closely. "Have you formed your soul connection?"

"Why do ya wanna know that?" I hedged, already suspecting what she was after. I had promised her I'd let her see me in my octopus form.

The eye roll she gave in response as she sipped her coffee, looking very at home on my sofa, didn't require words.

"Okay, I said I'd show ya what I looked like, but could you give me five minutes to enjoy what I've been craving for years?" She remained silent while I sorted the breakfast, taking the cups and plates to the small table and placing them down when I heard movement in the bedroom.

When I sat down and sipped the coffee, I met her gaze over the rim of my cup, lifting one brow at her inquisitive stare while enjoying the caffeine buzzing through me.

"I helped you and I'm dying to see what you look like. I've waited a long time too." She crossed her short-clad leg over her other knee, the foot bouncing and slapping her thongs against the sole of her foot. "I held out for years waiting to glimpse your tentacle friend."

"You what?" Shaun hissed from the bedroom doorway where he stood, dressed in last night's clothes, looking rumpled and smelling fresh.

How had I not heard him coming?

He wasn't looking at me, but directly at Mandy. "I'm getting the impression I'm missing something here." That was when he looked at me and I got a direct hit of uncertainty coming from him.

How did I explain myself?

Mandy rose and walked over to Shaun, while my mind raced to find the best way to explain my involvement in this mess. Her slim shoulders shrugged as she placed her cup down on the table she passed, her stare not moving from Shaun.

I decided to keep quiet, figuring they needed to sort this out between them. I'd learned a long time ago that getting between siblings was not the best idea. Despite that, deep down, I knew I should probably confess to what I'd done.

"I've known for about a decade that Fitch was... different."

"You knew!" His outrage came out in the snarl.

Looking unperturbed by Shaun's anger, she nodded. "Yep. I caught him using a tentacle to pull you in the water a long time ago."

"Why didn't you say something?"

I was trying to work out if it impressed Fitch she'd kept quiet about what she'd seen or pissed him off that she'd known something before him. It was a close call with what he was projecting at me.

"I wasn't totally sure, and you were so oblivious and, at fifteen, it was fun to know something you didn't." She nudged his shoulder. "Not so much now with how clueless you were to Fitch's obvious attraction to you and you pretending like Fitch wasn't the best thing since sliced bread."

He ran a hand through his damp hair, a scowl forming as lines deepened over his forehead. "You are so damn annoying! You know that, right?"

"It's in the sister's handbook," she replied, smiling widely as she glanced in my direction, making my stomach roll with apprehension. "So did you two…" her hands rose and waved in the air, "get jiggy with it?"

"None of your damn business," Shaun fired back, redder than the time he got sunburned one Christmas.

"I beg to differ. I helped you both and Fitch promised I could see his octopus."

Shaun's head flicked so fast in my direction, I was worried about whiplash. "You did what?"

Oh fuck! The screeching wasn't good. "Ya see—"

"Fuck, you did!"

Up and going to him, I pleaded, "I needed help to..."

He shook his head and I paused, realizing he had already read from my thoughts whatever I was about to say.

"You got Mandy to help!" His jaw flexed hard enough his teeth snapped together as he aimed a glare at Mandy. "You played us both."

"She did?" I asked, staring at his sister wide eyed and with the tiniest bit of pride at her devious antics.

"I played you both and look at you all happy and sex—"

"Don't!" Shaun snapped as he glanced at me. *I'm sorry.*

Why? We both fell for it. And she did help.

I just wasn't going to say it aloud with how smug she was looking right then.

Chapter Sixteen

Shaun

It was hard to stay angry at how Mandy manipulated us both to where we were now. Only if I didn't think about the night before and her need to humiliate me, though. Little Bo Peep would be an everlasting memory of horror that could compete with the scariest movies. Something I hoped to laugh about in the future.

"So, are we heading to the beach so I can see Fitch morph, or whatever it is you do, in the water?"

I sighed heavily when Fitch blushed and looked more interested in the food and coffee he'd returned to while I'd had a stare off with Mandy. "I think I should be the one to see Fitch... do his thing first and alone." It was the best I could come up with when I emphasized the first part, picking up mixed feelings from Fitch about the second aspect.

"I shift and I'm not sure either of ya should witness it."

"What!" said Mandy, giving Fitch a death glare.

"Why?" I asked at the same time. I didn't like the thought that he didn't want me to see him like that because he thought I might freak out.

"To answer ya both," he muttered, not looking at either of us, "it's not something I've done before."

"You have!" Mandy exclaimed, not letting Fitch off the hook. "I've seen you! Or have you forgotten?" The way she said it ensured if he said differently, he'd be lying.

Fitch looked as if he was about to burst into flames with how red he'd gotten and, feeling protective, I went to him, slipping an arm over his shoulder. "Leave him be, Mandy. This isn't 'bout you. If Fitch isn't comfortable shifting in front of you—"

"You mean us, not me, asshat. He isn't happy to shift in front of you either 'cause you act like a big sissy."

Fitch's head tipped back, his hair grazing my skin as he shook with laughter. "Children, stop squabbling," he spluttered between bouts of laughter. "Ya need to chill."

He pushed up from the chair, still chuckling, to move into my embrace more fully, his arm hooking around my waist. "I'll show ya both."

"You will?" I questioned when I could still feel something other than humor coming from him.

"Yep. Might as well get this out of the way now."

Okay, that didn't sound at all enthusiastic, but I let him go when he dropped his arm to step away. I watched him closely as he searched for a pair of thongs. Feet slapping, he walked to the door, holding it open. A wall of heat hit me and sweat gathered on my skin before we'd taken ten steps outside. My jeans were way too heavy for the blistering heat and I wished I'd not pushed to do this before going home to get changed.

Mandy peppered Fitch with questions as she walked at his side. I listened with my anxiety growing at thoughts of what I was about to witness.

Please don't freak out.

Please don't freak out.

Please don't freak out.

Fitch stopped as we got the stairs leading down to the part of the beach where the land was private. He met my stare with an unreadable expression that caused my stomach to recall how much alcohol I'd had the night before.

Had he picked up on my panic?

I didn't slap my forehead, but I wanted to when he clearly got I was having an anxiety attack at what was about to happen.

Ya can go back to the house.

There was nothing about how he'd said it to suggest that he'd be upset if I did. Thing was, I knew him better than I knew myself and doing that would hurt him. I shook my head, getting Mandy looking between us with interest. Her brows rose under her fringe while her hands went to her hips. "What am I missing here?"

"Nothing." The answer got her glowering at me. "It's too hot to be standing tongue wagging. Let's get to the water."

I encouraged them both down onto the sand, my feet sinking into the hot sand as the sparkling water held my attention. Fitch walked away from the crowded part of the beach nearest to where the boundary was for the private part of the beachfront.

As the sound of voices lessened, my tension increased. My shoulders felt stretched like an elastic band by the time we reached the small cove that jutted out and blocked the view of anyone potentially looking in our direction.

The silence felt as hot as the sun baking my head. Not a cloud drifted in the sky, allowing the vivid blue to create a line that highlighted the aquamarine of the water. Everything about the moment etched itself into my mind like so many other moments with Fitch. Only this was life changing, like the bite mark I wore on my skin that tugged at the sight of Fitch stripping without preamble.

"Mandy, look the other way, for pity's sake!" I grumbled at her interested stare. She laughed right at me, but turned when Fitch removed the rest of his clothes.

Gloriously naked, his bronzed skin glowed as the sun highlighted every beautiful inch of him. There was a vitality about him that had always held me captive. Was it the soul connection? Had a part of me recognized it, even as a child? He made everything else feel small and insignificant compared to him. He was mine. Had always been mine.

The biting, the touching were significant to how I was feeling, but the essence of what I felt for Fitch as that small boy underpinned the realness of who he was to my heart. Love had flooded every part of me in the month I spent with him every year. It sustained me in the following months of loneliness. Was I scared about what came next?

I stepped forward, knowing nothing would change how I felt about Fitch—absolutely nothing. I couldn't take my eyes off him as he entered the water, his body rippling. Tentacles appeared before my eyes but before I could admire him, he disappeared into the waves.

Fascination drew me to follow him. Everything else simply no longer mattered when Fitch's joy at how the water felt to him—to his octopus—came at me in waves of pleasure.

Before I realized it, I was reaching out to touch and experience Fitch in his natural habitat. Water soaked the material of my jeans, and I laughed when tentacles roamed up the leg of my jeans, tickling my skin.

Your octopus is playful.

I am.

I jerked at the voice that wasn't Fitch yet somehow was.

Can you talk to me? I shook my head at my stupidity. *Of course he can talk to me!*

Yes. We are soulmates. Our connection is everlasting. Nothing will break it, not even death.

Should that have freaked me out? Possibly. Yet I could only feel sorry for those who didn't have this special gift of eternity. The concept of never being alone, even in death, was awe-inspiring.

Can I touch you?

There were sounds of splashing, which I assumed was Mandy, only I didn't look away from the octopus wrapping itself around my jean clad calves. I knew what an octopus looked like from visiting aquariums yet somehow, seeing Fitch this way was like I'd never seen one before.

A large, elongated head merged into a brownish body with blue lines over it. They glowed brighter, and I recalled being told it was a warning of some kind.

If I touch you, will I get poisoned?

It was strange to hear laughter vaguely similar to Fitch's. *I'm poisonous, yes. But my venom is in your body now and it protects you. I can't harm you and neither can any other predator of the sea.*

Holy crap. You poisoned me!

My alarm came through, because I failed to keep my initial reaction to thoughts of being poisoned to myself. The screechy voice I'd used, although only in my head, didn't sound all that calm and collected to how I'd felt seconds before.

His amusement came across before he answered, *Yes. And if I recall correctly, you enjoyed the effects very much.*

Okay, I've just been called out by an octopus for my sexcapades. I seriously wasn't sure how to feel about that.

"He's beautiful."

Long tentacles moved further up my legs, almost as if they were dancing seductively in the water to show off to Mandy, who giggled like a child.

Rolling my eyes at her, I reached down and, for the first time, stroked a fingertip over a tentacle. Unsure what to expect, I wasn't prepared for the bolt of electricity to run through my mate's mark and down to my cock. I quickly angled my body away from Mandy when Fitch encouraged me to touch more of him.

"Do you think he'd let me touch him?"

"No," I snapped possessively before she'd taken half a step closer. A possessiveness to keep this man—octopus, solely mine, reared up with such violence it knocked me physically back two steps. It took an effort not to bare my teeth at my sister, despite her not being any threat.

"Hey, there's no need to get shirty with me!" Her snappy response was at odds with the knowing smirk she aimed at me.

"You wanted to see him and you have. Now bugger off and let us have a moment."

Fitch wanted me to... swim with him and I was eager to experience that too, only with fewer clothes. I didn't want an audience either.

"Ungrateful much," she said around her laughter as she splashed water on us before turning and wading back to the shoreline. There, she glanced back at me, a smile lighting her eyes. "I'm happy you both finally saw through the seaweed to the octopus."

I busted out a laugh at the awful pun as she waved and headed back up the beach.

What is she talking about?

I shrugged, then felt silly, unsure how good an octopus's vision was. *She's Mandy. There's no explaining her. Should I strip?*

Yes.

That was all Fitch, and I'd need to talk to him about this switching when he was—human—himself again. Fitch untangled himself from me, only making me aware I'd not stopped stroking him until he swam away to give me room. The sense of loss was immediate and I rushed to shuck my jeans, though that was harder with how the wet denim glued to my legs. I gave in and waded out to sit on the sand and yank them off, checking twice that no one was watching me before I stood naked and walked back into the ocean, straight to Fitch. Somehow, I could see exactly where he was, even as the blue was no longer as vibrant, and he blended more with the seabed.

It's our connection. It allows you to identify us when we are in the water.

Cool.

Water splashed around me as I walked deeper into the warm ocean. Sun bounced off the waves as they lapped at my skin while Fitch came and wrapped himself around my leg, his suckers teasing as he used them to move up my body. Tentacles stroked and explored, sucked and appeared to taste my skin by the sounds filling my head. The previous mention of beaks wasn't as bothersome with how gentle he was with me and how good the suction felt.

Beautiful.

Blushing at the sheer admiration I heard, I grazed fingertips over tentacles, hoping he could feel my emotions that I couldn't find a voice to communicate.

On and on he touched me, encouraging me to sink deeper into the water until I became fully submerged. Dipping my head under the water briefly, I watched how he propelled himself and me through the water.

Careful, I'm a strong swimmer, but won't have the same abilities as you.

With me, you have nothing to fear.

What do you mean?

Breathe under the water.

I surfaced, laughing while catching my breath. *I'm not a sea creature.*

No, but you are mated to one. Trust me.

My head wasn't so sure about what he was proposing, whereas my heart was fully engaged. I let it rule and dived under the next wave. *Here goes nothing.*

Bracing myself to find my lungs full of water, I inhaled.

Fitch's laughter rumbled inside my head as he reformed into the stunning man he was. His grin was huge.

See, ya fine.

I stared at him, memories of every time he'd coughed up a lung running through my head as I breathed, much like I did out of the water.

You've always been able to do this, I accused, my eyes narrowing on the playful man in front of me.

By this ya mean swim and breathe underwater?

I nodded and my hair floated about my head.

Yep.

Moving fast, he swam backwards out of my reach as I went to grab him, my confidence growing under the water. More laughter filled my head. *You are gonna need to be quicker than that.*

With no need to surface, I could see the advantages as I darted left before sweeping back and wrapping my arms around Fitch. Silky skin ran up against mine and his groan matched mine as he twisted to face me. His lips fused to mine and any thoughts about how easy it was to kiss under water slipped from my mind when his tongue ran along the seam of my lips, encouraging me to open. To deepen the kiss. A saltiness that was no stronger than usual filled my mouth as his tongue tangled with mine. A hand roamed up my back, reaching the base of my skull, holding me the way he wanted.

Tentacles moved, supporting my limbs. I acknowledged somewhere in the back of my mind, while the kiss brought forward the passion that had been interrupted by Mandy earlier, that I was making out in the sea. Under the water.

Legs intertwined, Fitch brought his body flush against mine, causing a groan to rumble at the delicious rub of silky smooth skin against mine. His hips rocked to stroke his erection up my hard length. I swallowed the sounds he made, or though I did. I wasn't sure because everything felt so out of my element.

Water teased as it slipped between us with each maddening undulation of Fitch's body. Tentacle suckers slid over my backside. They sucked at the flesh, sending shivers of pleasure directly to my cock, which pulsed against Fitch's. Desperately wanting more, I attempted to slip a hand between us, my intention to stroke our cocks together. Next thing I knew, a tentacle wrapped around my cock and the suckers did this weird little move of a stroke and suck at the same time.

I wrenched my mouth from his, gasping, yet not short of breath. It was fucking weird, only not enough to get me to want to stop as I stared at him with unbelievable sensations bombarding my cock. The suckers were a lot like mouths nibbling on my cock. It was insanely hot to think of Fitch with multiple mouths.

Why the heck was I scared of suckers?

Who cares when ya came to your senses?

I met his chuckle with a groan at the tightening of the surrounding tentacles, while the ones touching my backside traveled down the crease of my ass. I gasped when tentacles released me, then returned, bringing Fitch's cock to join the party.

I was gasping and groaning, mouth open, it registered somewhere in my head, but the pleasure kept me from considering that too hard. The tentacles holding our cocks squeezed and this unusual sensation followed, much like our cocks had a mouth around them. Eyes rolling into the back of my head, hips swaying and rocking into the delicious sensation, I threw back my head. A groan got swept away in the waves as a sucker latched onto my asshole and wriggled. At the heady feelings of bliss building in my sac, it left me crying out mindlessly.

Gonna come!

A throbbing ache in my cock pushed the cum physically up my length as Fitch filled my head with how much he wanted to be inside me, just as a tentacle breached my ass.

Oh fuck! God yeah, so tight. Look at me.

Impossible to ignore the pleading command, I met his heated stare. His eyes glowed with pleasure and sucked me right into their depth, sending my orgasm spiraling out of control. Hips jerking at the tentacle rubbing my g-spot, his body was the only thing stopping me from sinking to the ocean floor. Cum pulsed violently from me, my body seized as I felt his love roll through me. A brightness filled my mind, a heady color that bathed me and stole my ability to do more than embrace this man who'd always held my heart. *Mine. You are mine.*

Always.

His cock pulsed hard against mine as he opened himself more, letting me experience his joy at having waited for this moment to happen. His heated stare drew every drop of pleasure from my balls until they were empty.

Spent, I clung to him with the knowledge he wouldn't let anything happen to me.

Unable to say how long we floated under the water before he lazily propelled us to the surface, I blinked the water out of my eyes at the brightness of the sun. The heat was a sharp contrast to being under the cooler water.

I rested my head on his shoulder as the waves carried us closer to the shore. "How did I get so lucky?" The level of seriousness in my voice brought a furrow between Fitch's brows when he shifted to look directly into my face.

"I'm the one who won the lotto, for sure, the day we met."

It was corny, and I'd probably rag on his ass for his comment, but right now, all I could do was grin like a Cheshire Cat. "Is that so? In that case, can you..." I looked to where the shore was, then back at my octopus, "get us back to shore under tentacle speed?"

His hair was darker and plastered to his skull, and water glittered like diamonds on his eyelashes. He'd never looked more attractive to me when he quirked his head to the side, narrowing his eyes, a mischievous glint appearing in their depth. "Tentacle speed?"

It was an obvious question, but I'd no time to answer as he enfolded me in his tentacles, then we moved through the water so fast I couldn't blink away the water spray blurring my vision.

What felt like mere seconds later, I was on the wet sand with a laughing Fitch lying next to me. "Fast enough for ya?"

I twisted my head towards him as I sat up, sand sticking to my salty, wet skin. My heart swelled with affection for the man lying next to me, chest heaving, gloriously naked. His flaccid cock held my lingering gaze. My own thickened at thoughts of touching him.

I glanced up and down the beach to make sure no one could spy on us before I reached out. Tracing a finger over droplets of water, his skin pebbled, and he shivered. A low moan followed at the touch of the tip of his cock. His eyelids fluttered and enlarging pupils darkened his eyes until they lost all color as he held my stare. I ran a fingertip down the length of his cock, watching how his breathing sped up, coming in small gasps.

When I reached the base and moved back up the growing thickness, a drop of pre-cum glistened at his slit.

With one more check up and down the beach, I bent over him and engulfed the head of his cock between my lips, sucking the head deep into the cavern of my mouth. Saltiness coated my tongue, which oddly combined the sea and Fitch. It was addicting and I couldn't see how a lifetime together would be enough for me to get my fill!

Chapter Seventeen

Fitch

The cry of a bird startled me awake and I sat up, dazed. The height of the sun in the clear blue sky showed it was late afternoon. I glanced about, confused. I had no recollection of how I got from the water's edge up the beach near home. Or how I was in my bathers, on my swag, with an esky sat next to me and no sign of Shaun.

I sank back into the swag, my arm falling over my face, shielding my eyes from the bright, fiery ball above me. By the smell and feel of my skin, Shaun had taken good care of me. I didn't need sunscreen as I didn't burn, something else Shaun didn't know about me.

I exhaled noisily.

There were so many things about me I'd not shared. A grin slowly spread over my lips at how that would no longer be an issue. He'd not freaked out... *he'd not freaked out at all!*

Letting that settle for a moment, now the previous night's alcohol consumption couldn't take the blame for my actions, I took stock of how I was feeling. I'd gotten used to the ball of anxiety that came with being close to Shaun and not being able to voice my feelings or explain about our connection. To find it gone was monumental. The need to find him got me sitting back up, my nose filtering the scents. I glanced over my shoulder and the sight of Shaun strolling towards me made my heart rate pick up and leave me breathless.

"Hey sleepyhead," Shaun called out, a sexy smile morphing over his beautiful face.

Sun cream glistened on his broad chest and black bathers hung off his slim hips. He carried a large plate of what smelled like snags, which caused my stomach to snarl and reminded me it needed feeding. Only, as I watched him stroll over the sand, his stare holding mine, my desire for food changed to something way tastier—Shaun.

His grin widened with all the cheekiness I loved, increasing my need to taste him. "This mind connection thing we got going, it sure makes things easier. Only problem is, if you think those dirty thoughts, I don't know how safe I'll be around you and my family. Dude, you gotta stop that!"

Matching his smile when he came to sit next to me, I smelled his arousal. "Then we'll just have to spend our time alone so as not to offend anyone."

Laughter shook his body as he offered me a snag. "Put that in your mouth and behave. Your mom and dad are coming down with the rest of the food. And Mandy and my parents are joining us, too."

Seeing as he was serious, I scowled and took a bite of the snag as I eyed him. "Why? And a quickie. How did I get," I pointed to my bathers, after swallowing what was in my mouth, "in these and up on my swag?"

"You passed out cold after you got your rocks off a second time when I wiggled my finger in..." he came in close, his lips brushing my ear as he whispered, "your ass and sucked you dry."

The groan was low and needy; it went with the ache forming in my balls at the flood of memory of exactly what he'd done to me.

"Ya cruel fucker," I muttered at the glimpse I caught of my parents coming onto the beach with his family following behind, making it impossible to give in to the temptation that was Shaun.

I bit his ear, hard enough to leave an imprint.

"Hey!" A scowl dug lines around his eyes as he pulled away and rubbed at his earlobe. "Was there any need, *dude*?"

"Every," I directed at him, before raising my knees up to hide the effect he'd had on me and shouting at Mom, "what's this?"

"What does it look like?" she called back, looking awfully pleased with herself as she approached.

"That you are having a party," I replied once I eyed what she was carrying. I groaned in complaint when it struck what we were planning on celebrating. "Why can't I have normal parents?"

"'Cause ya special," Dad answered, laughing at me.

Shaun didn't appear phased by the idea of a party to celebrate our mating. I stared at him, eyes narrowing. *How long were ya in the house alone with my parents? And what did ya talk about?*

A while and nothing you need to worry about.

Eyes widening, I turned my attention back to my parents, knowing them as I did, I glared. "Do ya want to scare Shaun off? What did ya tell him?"

Two sets of eyes offered nothing as I glanced between them, wanting to hurry the conversation along before Shaun's family reached us. Mandy knowing was one thing, but his parents... yeah, I wasn't sure they'd want me in their family if they knew the truth.

They know.

Turning my attention back to Shaun, I stared at him with disbelieving eyes. *Are ya shitting me?*

No. It seems your parents told them some time ago.

I looked back at my parents. Dad shrugged, seemingly fully aware of my conversation with Shaun, or the gist of it, anyway. "Son, we're happy for ya both. We wanted to make sure there were no surprises." Dad smiled and patted my shoulder. "Now who wants what thrown on the grill? Ya must be starvin'."

I didn't buy the innocent look he gave me, or how Shaun smothered his laughter with the back of his hand while looking away. "I'll have whatever ya got," I replied, keeping a watchful eye on everyone.

What did ya tell them while I was sleeping?

Nothing. Absolutely nothing. Shaun grabbed a stubby out of the esky and handed it to me. *To help you cool off...* he winked saucily, a fingertip stroking over my hand.

I'll get ya back later, teasing fucker.

"Someone wanna help with this esky?" Mandy asked, stopping the conversation for now.

Shaun darted to help and then help his parents get sorted with the large shade sail they used to protect themselves from the sun. Once finished setting up, Shaun came back and parked himself next to me, stubby in hand. He leaned his shoulder against mine and made a sound that was pure contentment.

Mandy, who'd placed herself under the shade sail, cast a glance in our direction as she spoke in a faint voice to her mom. Something about the look she wore made my nerves thrum. The feeling increased as she pulled her shoulder bag closer and dug inside, bringing her phone out. A second later, tensing at the sound of music and laughter coming from the phone, I shook my head. "Oh gods, ya filmed us!"

Shaun seemed to understand what I was getting at when he got up so fast he kicked sand everywhere in his hurry to get to Mandy. Only it was too late. Everyone had crowded around Mandy, staring down at the screen as I heard Shaun's voice shouting, "Are we ready to get crazy? Let me introduce my sidekick... Little Miss Red Riding Hood."

I could recall the laughter and catcalls, with cries of 'yes'. What also popped into my head was what came next and I buried my face in my knees. "Make that tight ass dance for the crowd," Shaun called out over the noise in the background, and I had because I loved him.

Mom's laughter drowned out some of the noise and I fucking hoped that was the worst of what Mandy had captured.

"Son, I didn't know ya had those moves in ya."

Head popping up, I glared at the group huddled around Mandy. "Unless ya want to be traumatized for the rest of ya life, I'd stop watching now," I said, adding enough fatalism to my voice to make my point.

"Ohhhh—"

"Mom, don't... please," I begged, knowing she could and would rival Mandy when she got going.

Peals of laughter rang out and I gave Mandy a warning look, one I figured she'd ignore.

Shaun, quick as a flash, had the phone out of her hand and was running off in the direction of the steps leading up off the beach, Mandy giving chase. "Gimme that back, asshole."

"Language," her mom shouted after her, rolling her eyes, the smile remaining.

I watched Shaun disappear. It was easier to pretend interest in him than the four other people that were all staring at me. At least it felt like it with how I was sweating at the attention.

In the end, I gave up and shifted my attention to the group of grinning fools. "What?"

Shaun's mom came over and sat next to me, slipping an arm around my waist, something she'd done a thousand times over the years. She leaned in and kissed my cheek. A few seconds passed as she met my worried stare. "You were always part of our family from the first moment you made my son smile. He was only ever truly happy with you, and it makes my heart content to see that you both have accepted the love between you." She placed another kiss on my hot cheek. "I wish you both a life of happiness and love."

"I'm just glad they got me as a sister, otherwise they'd never have gotten their heads out of their asses," Mandy shouted breathlessly as she ran back towards us, clearly having heard the conversation. The phone was nowhere in sight.

Aiming to keep the amusement at her to myself, I narrowed my eyes, aiming for a frown. "Gloating, much! Self-praise ain't no praise!"

"Children," Mom said at the same time as Shaun's mom.

They laughed at each other. Shaun's mom got up and dusted off the sand Shaun had kicked over her, going to help Mom with the food and everything was right back to the way it always was. Nothing had changed, yet for me everything had. Shaun was mine.

You bet your scrawny ass you are.

Who are ya callin' scrawny?

You.

Bring ya ass back here and I'll show ya what this scrawny ass can do.

The threat brought a wave of lust that was hard to shove aside when Shaun sent images of exactly how he'd like my ass.

Seeing this could turn dangerous with everyone on the beach with me, I shut Shaun out and tuned back into the conversation where Christmas was the focus.

"Is Kev coming over for the Christmas beach party?" Mom asked Mandy, who was in the process of filling a plastic cup with wine.

"Think so. He mentioned something about a gift."

"A gift... must be serious." I gave her an innocent smile. "Ya must be good in—"

"Don't even," Mandy snapped at me with a killer glare.

"What?" I asked, feigning innocence. "Ya were happy to want to see me and Shaun getting it on."

"Mandy," her mom scolded. "You didn't!"

"No, I didn't," she aimed at her mom while glaring at me. "I was messing with the two lug heads, is all."

"Sounded like you meant it at the time."

"Kev wants to know how the costumes got damaged?" she replied, grinning maniacally at me, making me sweat once more as I tried to think of something that would explain their state.

"Have ya seen the size of the outfits next to me and Shaun? You try getting out of them!"

"Good point... and talking about outfits, what did you buy for Shaun this year?"

My lips twitched at the gift I'd bought for Shaun and wrapped to place under the Christmas tree. A gag gift. One I'd bought in the hope I'd have the courage to confess what I was, not that it was necessary any more. Should I get him something else?

We'd agreed to wear whatever the other bought for Christmas a long time ago and had worked to outdo each other every year since. Normally it was bathers with some awful design and material. He'd found a knitted pair of bathers a couple of years ago, so far neither of us had beat it for awfulness. I'd memories of when I'd come out of the sea with the wool stretching down to my ankles and enormous gaps in the wool revealing my junk. At the memory of my humiliation, I grinned to myself and decided I had Shaun beat this year.

Mandy caught my gaze, a shaped brow rising. "What you plotting over there? How bad is it?"

I glanced up the beach to check Shaun hadn't somehow snuck up on me. "Let's just say... it's tentastical."

She spluttered with laughter. "This year, I'm gonna make sure I'm up to see his reaction. I've a feeling I won't want to miss it!"

Grinning at her, I nodded in agreement. "Make sure ya phone is recording."

Chapter Eighteen

Fitch

Heaven, I'd often wondered, as I lay staring up at the night sky, if it held as many wonders as the ocean did for me. It held none of my attention with the feel of Shaun's tongue circling the head of my cock. A groan tore from my chest as that wicked appendage darted into my slit and Shaun made a noise somewhere between a groan and gasp that lodged right in my balls. They tightened with desire as I thrust up as he drew off me, making me curse and beg for more. "Please... fuck... stop teasing me!"

Wet lips brushed over the head of my cock and under the light of the moon, I could only see a glint in Shaun's eyes. However, I could feel every bit of his amusement at my desperation.

Weeks had passed since we'd claimed each other and nothing quelled the need inside me when he touched me. His kisses, whether or not he intended them to, set me alight quicker than a match to a torch.

His talented tongue traveled my throbbing length, then licked around the base. His nose buried into my balls as I felt him inhale before he sucked them into his mouth. That same delightful tongue slipped around them while the noises he made vibrated through me, sending sparks to ignite in my lower belly.

My fingers dug into the sand as hands held my thighs open and against my swag beneath. A slurping sound followed when his lips popped off my balls, spit dripping down his chin, which glistened in the moonlight. He moved to rub his face back in my groin. The scruff on his jaw abraded my skin and added to the torment of desire coiled at the base of my spine like a brown snake waiting to strike. Everywhere ached with the longing to be filled.

He worked me over until it strung me out. His large hand cupped my balls, lifting them as his nose moved down the crease of my thigh until I felt wetness trace over my taint. The sounds he made as his tongue got frisky with my ass made me want to bust a nut. Only I wanted him inside me when that happened.

He had this ability to make all other thoughts slip from my brain when he touched me and so far, I'd not had the pleasure of more than his tongue or finger in my ass. I'd planned tonight, brought lube, and he wasn't going to derail me. The ache increased at the feel of his tongue dipping and circling my hole and my body pushed into the touch, desperately looking for more. Needing more. Needing everything.

"Please... fuck me..." I gasped, begging for what I'd craved for years.

The slick tongue pressed against the right rim of muscle, and I reached down to squeeze the base of my cock at nerve endings buzzing with pleasure that came with an indescribable burn. It moved from my tailbone through my body to short-circuit my brain once more.

"No... shit... fuck... want more..." I stuttered, eyes slamming shut as I attempted to wriggle back and away, when it was the last thing my body wanted.

Balmy air blew over my oversensitive skin as the tongue disappeared and I felt Shaun's stare sear through my skin. "Are you sure? I'm happy to wait—"

I groaned at the sincerity. My virginity status hung between us, and Shaun continued to hold back. I sensed how much he wanted me, but also the need to make this about me. Both were heady and though initially I'd let him go at a slower pace, it wasn't enough now. "I need ya inside me in the worst way." Scrabbling to reach for where I'd stashed the lube in my swag, I released another groan of approval when I found it.

I threw the bottle at him.

"Woah! You could have taken my eye out," he exclaimed dramatically, two seconds before he burst out laughing.

Too needy for more, my laughter sounded like a hyena. "It's your fault for getting me so damn wound up."

I could hear the snick of the lid opening as I held my breath and continued to ring the base of my cock, unsure I'd last two seconds once he got inside me.

"Breathe for me, Fitch," he whispered softly as a slicked fingertip stroked over my hole.

A shiver ran through me at the difference between the coolness of the lube and the warmth of Shaun's skin. Slowly he circled over the puckered flesh, gentle caresses causing the air to release from my chest in quick pants.

My thighs widened invitingly. Shaun didn't need a second invite and came closer. The night sky didn't let me see more than shadows of his reflection. His intentions came from the gentleness of each caress. From how I felt his presence in my mind as he pushed the lubed finger into my ass, sharing how it felt to be inside me.

My cock throbbed painfully, and I tightened my hold, not wanting to come before he had more than a finger inside me.

"I can feel how much you want me," he murmured, a deep sense of satisfaction there in every word he spoke.

"I do. Want ya so badly. I feel like I can't breathe."

His groan as my ass clamped down got him moving deeper, stroking over the walls of my ass, searching. He hit my g-spot and I panted, desperately working to think of something other than what he was doing to me.

Tentacles formed out of my free hand and I reached for the fallen lube bottle, needing a distraction. As naked as me from our late Christmas-eve swim, I easily slipped a tentacle between his legs, stroking around his balls.

"Motherfucker!" he moaned. "Fitch, you aren't playin' fair."

Suckers latched over his hole and I sent him the image of how it looked from the last time I'd made him come like this. "Then stop teasing me with one finger!"

Laughter came quickly, followed by a groan when I increased the suction as he removed his finger to replace it with two. The burn increased as he pushed in slowly, the overload of lube on his hand easing the feeling as the pressure increased. Doing as he said earlier, I took some slow, even breaths, letting my body adjust.

The moment I relaxed, Shaun withdrew, then pushed back in. "So tight, hot, and silky. I could live here for days and never tire." As if to prove his point, he left his fingers where they were, stroking deep, then moved up over me to claim a kiss.

Tongue and teeth clashed at the desperate need between us. I wasn't sure whose need I could feel, but it didn't matter. Hunger. A monster with a thirst for pleasure tore at the frayed edges of my sanity and I rocked on the fingers in my ass, squeezing hard.

Grunts and cries carried on the night air as hands grappled with tentacles as desire became hotter than the surface of the sun. It burned until nothing else mattered. Just the need to have Shaun in me, on me, anyway I could have him.

Incoherent noises fell from my parted lips as my vision wavered at the first touch of Shaun's cock pressing against my slick hole. The muscle quivered at the pressure against my rim as large hands cupped my head, fingers sinking into my hair.

"Breathe out," he murmured, his tongue moving over my parted lips. His own breathing came in short bursts.

Doing as he asked, he pushed into me. One slow steady move, his gaze holding mine. His heart was open, along with his mind about how he felt.

There was everything I'd ever wanted. Love. Enough to fill several oceans.

Tears gathered at the corner of my eyes as he reverently kissed my lips. "I was always a sucker for Christmas *because of you*."

My response caught in my throat as he moved deeper in my ass, ripping away the last remnant of control I had.

I cried out into the night, loving how corny my guy could be as above us, fireworks exploded in the night sky, raining color over us, revealing it was midnight.

They wasted the spectacular show on me when Shaun was relentless, wringing every ounce of pleasure from me. His fingers clung on as he rolled his hips, thrusting deeper and harder. His dewy skin glided over my cock repeatedly, adding to the ripples of pleasure with each brush of his cock to my g-spot.

Imagining it and experiencing it... fuck, they were worlds apart.

It'll get better, too, he whispered in my mind as he kissed down my throat until his lips reached my mate mark, then Shaun's mouth widened. Teeth struck their mark and the night exploded. Cum erupted from my body until I lay limp against the swag, breathlessly trying to figure out how long it would take for my body to recover, and when we could take that wild ride again.

There's no rush. His laughter sounded sleepy as he relaxed more fully against me, crushing me into the swag beneath.

Says who?

Me.

I grinned while my ass twinged when he shifted a little, as if to get more comfortable, and his cock slipped free from my body. He could be right about waiting... except there was always his ass, too!

Behave.

Why? Weren't you the one who said ya were 'a sucker for Christmas'? And it's officially Christmas day. Tentacles moved over the sand, searching as Shaun grunted next to my ear, unmoving.

My grin widened when I found the bottle. Twisting my head to look at Shaun as best as I could with his face buried in my swag, I kissed the cheek I could reach. "I think I need to test that theory out..."

His head lifted and his face inched close enough I could feel his breath on my sweaty skin. "Is that so?"

I slipped the now lubed tentacle between his buttocks, chuckling at his moan and the plumping cock resting against my thigh. "Ya love my suckers."

"That I do." He removed the small distance between us, his lips trailing over mine softly. "Now, let's see exactly what they're capable of."

~/~/~/~

Shaun

We'd had a later start than normal because of our late night antics on the beach. It had taken two showers to rid us of all the sand that glued itself to our bodies with the amount of lube we'd got covered in.

I'd picked up Fitch's excitement when we'd finished brunch, and everyone had gathered to open presents. I'd considered myself prepared for whatever he'd found funny that kept him chuckling. Our one-upmanship was longstanding on gag gifts. My jaw went lax while I stared at the ugliness of the thing I held.

The clatter Mandy made as she literally laughed herself off the seat and fell on the floor, gasping, "try it on," through bouts of laughter, clutching her sides, made me flip her the bird.

"You try it on," I fired back, shifting my gaze back to the blue tentacled onesie. *Where the hell did you find this?*

Does it matter?

I glanced at my unrepentant boyfriend, giving him a hard stare. "Yep, it does!"

"Mom, tell him to stop doing the mind talking. It's not fair!" Mandy complained, getting up off the floor and stepping closer to inspect what I held. The oversized Christmas T-shirt she wore slipped off one shoulder.

"You're just jealous." I gave her a smug smile, knowing that would wind her up. The present in my hands got forgotten for a moment. It hadn't taken Mandy long to figure we could communicate in this way when it was easy to forget and start talking aloud halfway through a conversation. As she and the family knew about Fitch, I'd been open about the benefits... *just not all of them.*

Ya think my tentacles have benefits? He wagged his brows and gave me a suggestive leer. *Is that a remake of 'friends with benefits', thing?*

Always!

The clout to the side of my head got my attention returning to Mandy. Though she'd been gentle, I shouted, "ouch," knowing it would annoy Mom.

"Mandy, behave. And keep your hands to yourself," Mom stated in a firm, no nonsense tone that we both knew better than to argue with.

Back to grinning at her, she pointed to what I held. "Isn't it time to try on your present?"

Smile slipping, I scowled at how Fitch nodded his agreement. I stood, feeling a sense of doom as I eyed the clothes I'd slipped on when I'd gotten out of bed. I quickly realized I couldn't use an excuse to get changed and assess the awfulness of the tentacle outfit alone.

"It's not that bad, come on," Fitch encouraged, mischief lighting his eyes.

"Then maybe you should try it first... you being an octopus."

His laughter matched Mandy's. "Wooly bathers, that's all I'm sayin'!"

Every pair of eyes in the room watched as I stepped into the powder blue onesie, the tentacles floating about my body as I pulled it up my body. Everyone drowned out the Christmas music in the background as the room filled with raucous laughter.

Never looking more radiant, Fitch stared at me with all the happiness he felt, and I gave in to his joy. I flipped up the hood saying 'fuck it' when Fitch busted out in fits of laughter as I waggled the enormous goggle eyes back and forth.

"In my head, ya looked so much hotter," he stuttered, gasping for breath, eyes watering.

"See, you are just the same as me!" Mandy pointed at Fitch, getting groans from both our parents. "Fitch got his very own sucker for Christmas."

There was total silence for a brief second before everyone groaned except for Fitch, who continued to laugh uproariously.

Slipping my arm around my shaking boyfriend, I shook my head. "If you can't beat them, I might as well join them. What about... all I want for Christmas is tentacles? Or... tentacles and other stocking stuffers? No. No, I got it... twelve days of squidmus." Through the laughter, I continued, "It's a tenta-ful life," I spluttered around the fingers now clamped to my mouth.

"Enough," Fitch said through his snorting chuckles.

Licking at his fingers, I tasted his salt essence, and grinned. "Okay, I'll stop," I mumbled around his fingers. *For now. All bets are off when we're naked and you are—*

Don't ya dare.

A—

No...

Sucker—

Ass!

I nodded at him, because I was, and he loved me anyway. *For Christmas.*

His hand slipped away, and he kissed me softly. *No, for a*lways.

I can live with that.

The End....

This is the end for these too but if you want more tentacles check out the rest of the series listed below.

Tinsel and Tentacles Series

All I Want for Christmas is Tentacles - Chloe Archer
Tentacles and Other Stocking Stuffers - Delaney Rain

Tentacles Rock - K. C. Carmine

A Sucker for Christmas - JP Sayle

Jingle Bells and Elder Gods - Kiernan Kelly

Kraken Klaus - Charlotte Brice

Twelve Days of Squidmas - K.L. Hiers

Tentacle Wonderland - Reese Morrison

It's a Tenta-ful Life - Amanda Meuwissen

Rebel Without a Claus - Author L Eveland

Cthulhu for Christmas - Meghan Maslow

Series Link: https://mybook.to/TinselAndTentacles

About the Author

Eccentric cake lover who has a passion for words of all kinds. I'm Jayne or JP, I live in the Isle of Man. A tiny place in the Irish sea where all the magic happens. I'm a confessed bookaholic and if I'm not writing I love to snuggle with a book or two...if you catch my drift.

If you're interested in keeping up to date, then I've a few places you can do that, and they're listed below. My website is where you'll find all the different Me's there are, LOL. As I travel this path into the future, I'm going to be writing in different genres so to stop there being any confusion I'll be writing under different pen names.

If you would like to give me any feedback or just have any questions, go ahead and friend me on Facebook, and I would be happy to answer anything. I hope you enjoyed this book and if you would also like to leave a review, then I would love to read your thoughts. Even if you just want to rate it, I'll be grateful

Thank you for being a part of my dream.

Newsletter Sign up

Goodreads

Tumblr

Bookbub

Instagram

Twitter

Facebook

Website address

Facebook Author page

JP Manx Minx's

Patreon

Other books by the Author

Standalone

When Fake Changed Everything

Christmas beyond Christmas

The Elves and the Bondage Daddy (Grim and Sinister Delights Book 5)

Agrippa My Heart

His Boy to Tease

Headshot

A Brat For Kinkmas

A Little Christmas: Terrence

Hanging With Daddy

Music & Dreams: Rocktoberfest

Series

Assassins To Order With Lisa Oliver

Marvin – Marvin and Ajani

Ben – Ben, Teilo & Nico

Duron – Duron & Beaumont

Conrad – Conrad & Kylo

Dancing with the Devil – Wyatt & James

Tangled Tentacles Series with Lisa Oliver

Alexi #1

Victor #2

Todd #3

Markov # 4

Kelvin # 5

Little Paws Haven Series

Little Treasure he Hides

The Potters Creek Series

A Christmas Wish (book one)

The App Series

The App: Daddy kink (book one)

The App: Littles (book two)

The App: Puppy play (book three)

The Flamingo Bar Series

Always More (book one)

The Little Side of Me (book two)

3 Is the Magic Number (book three)

La Trattoria Di Amore Series

Puzzle Pieces (book one)

Dominated but not Subdued (book two)

Made to Submit

The Playroom Series

Mine, Body and Soul: Part One

Mine, Body and Soul: Part Two

Mine, Body and Soul: Part Three

Ferron's Journey: Damaged Part One (book four)

Ferron's Journey: Hidden Part Two (book five)

Ferron's Journey: Revelation Part Three (book six)

Mine, Body and Soul Trilogy

Ferron's Journey Trilogy

Spinoff Love's Heart Print

Dark River Stone Collective Series

The Light Beneath the Dark (Book One)

When Darkness Turns to Light (Book Two)

Running From Darkness (Book Three)

The Billionaire Playground Series

Property of a Billionaire (Book one)

Reluctant Billionaire (Book two)

Billionaire's Muse (Book three)

Heart Stones Series

Blood King

The Manx Cat Guardians Series Where it all Began: Origins (Book 1)
Seeing Beyond the Scars (Book 2)
Destiny Collides Past and Present (Book 3)
Searching for a Soul to Love (Book 4)
The 12 Disasters of Christmas (Book 5)
Laws of Attraction (Book 6)
The Teacher's Boy (Book 7)
Boxset

Audio Books

Mine, Body and Soul, Part One: The Playroom Series

Mine, Body and Soul, Part Two: The Playroom Series

Mine, Body and Soul, Part Three: The Playroom Series

Daddy Kink: The App (book one)

Always More: The Flamingo Bar (book one)

When Fake Changed Everything

Ferron's Journey: Damaged Part One

Ferron's Journey: Hidden Part Two

Ferron's Journey: Revelation Part Three

Romance books in a mixed series of M/F and M/M by the Author under a different pen name Jayne Paton

Smith's Corner

Delilah & Dallas (book one)

Layla & Levi (Book two)

Ash & Alora (Book three)

Fox & Faith (book four)

Storm & Stone (book five)

Hunter & Holden (book six)

Crime and Thrillers by the Author under a different pen name J Paton

Headspace

Chozen: Dark MM Crime Drama (Headspace Book 1)

Chozen: Dark MM Crime Drama (Headspace Book 2)